D1629749

000002205978

Jasmine Days

Jasmine Days

Benyamin

Translated from Malayalam by
Shahnaz Habib

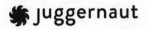 juggernaut

JUGGERNAUT BOOKS
KS House, 118 Shahpur Jat, New Delhi 110049, India

First published in Malayalam as *Mullappoo Niramulla Pakalukal*
by DC Books in 2014
First published by Juggernaut Books 2018

10 9 8 7 6 5 4 3

ISBN 9789386228741

Typeset in Adobe Caslon Pro by R. Ajith Kumar, New Delhi

Printed at Manipal Technologies Limited

Dedicated to those who were defeated,
in life and in revolution

Allah will not change the condition of a people till they change their own condition.

Quran, Ar-Ra'd 11

We must wash our eyes with darkness to see what we want to see.

Thomas Mann, *The Magic Mountain*

Jasmine Days

Sameera Parvin

Translated by Benyamin
from the original in Arabic titled
A Spring without Fragrance

To my baba

Contents

Part 1

Orange Radio

RJ

I sat again in front of the microphone for my beloved live programme, Rush Hour. It had been three months since I was in the studio.

No one had expected me to go live as soon as I returned, or for that matter, even return. Maybe that is why our programme manager, Imthiaz sir, told me, 'You don't have to go live if you are not up for it, just record something.' He was trying to be kind, but it made me sadder.

To not go live? Is that why I returned to the studio even though taya and my chachas told me not to? Is that why I asked the studio to announce my return even when they were hesitant? Does Sameera give in that easily?

For the last one week, the studio had been airing ads announcing my return. Since then listeners had been calling and texting and emailing the studio to express their delight. I could not disappoint them. They are my strength. My grief is my own secret. But in public, I am RJ Sameera. I pour happy words into my audience's ears, ask nonsense questions and listen to sweet nothings. That's the Sameera whose return they are looking forward to. And that is what made me get back into the live studio.

Still, I didn't like my intros to the first two songs. It was as if that old Sameera who turned into a river of talk in front of the microphone had run aground. I stumbled over some words and misspoke some names. I even asked Kapil bhai at the keyboard if he would write a couple of sentences for the next song. But bhai was confident. 'Don't worry, you will be fine by the next song.' He knew that I never prepped my intros. I would just listen to the song and improvise. That was my style. And that's why even two years after my programme began, Rush Hour still had excellent ratings.

Kapil bhai was right. By the third song I was back on track. My listeners were eating out of my hands. They welcomed me back happily. Some of them reproached me for taking such a long holiday. Others wanted to know if I had a fun vacation. Yet others wanted to know where I had gone on my holiday. I gave them answers they loved. I laughed with them, played with them, flirted with them. The hour-long show was about to wind up. Just then a live listener asked, 'So what news at home? Are your baba and mama doing well?' 'Yes, yes, they are well, very well,' I said, choking down a wild scream.

Each listener is different. It's hard to guess what might come out of which mouth. They all have demands that go beyond radio time. Some want my cellphone number. Others want to chat by email. Some ask for a photo. Some want to meet in person. Of course, there are always those who are looking for a romance. And the ones who want to marry me. And the ones who want nothing less than my body. I still remember one of my listeners; he always sent SMSs to my programme. Then he started calling regularly. Poor guy. He was a security guard at a construction site, somewhere far away from the city. My songs and chatter kept him going through his lonely days. I always had words of comfort for him. One day, during a live show, he started crying. He said he loved me and could no longer live without me. For a moment, I was tongue-tied. Then I took a deep breath and told him that he must love me like a daughter. My words calmed him and that day, in the office, as well as outside, many compliments came my way for my level-headed answer.

A good RJ never loses her cool whatever the provocation during a live show. I had always passed that test with A+. And yet today, I was taken aback by a standard question. The truth is, it shook me. Even though my listener kept talking, I couldn't respond. Kapil bhai was gesturing at me from beyond the glass wall to say something, anything. There was silence for a brief while. Radio is not like TV; a moment's silence can seem as long as a century. Kapil bhai put a song on to cover up. I couldn't stay in the studio any longer. I took off my headphones and left, not bothering to even finish the programme.

There was nobody else in the studio at that time. The station was to air a recorded programme for the next two hours. The morning programme was over and most of the staff had finished for the day. The rest were in the canteen. I sat down and closed my eyes. It's best to be alone when you are sad. I wanted to be by myself and feel my strength slowly seeping back into me.

After a while – I lost track of time – I felt a hand on my shoulder. It was Fathima Syed, the head of advertising.

She had been absent during the morning commotion, I remembered then. The moment I had stepped into the studio in the morning, everyone had crowded around me. They engulfed me with sympathy and love. Some stood nearby silently, hands folded across their torso. Others offered words of consolation. Some expressed their sorrow. Yet others were angry on my behalf. Philip Mathew sir, who went by the nickname Sheela Garments in office, patted my head as if I were his daughter. Everyone got a pale smile from me in return. Our station manager John Maschinas offered me a formal condolence and returned to his cabin. I appreciated that. Not much else was necessary after all. All those other gestures of sympathy seemed a little melodramatic to me. My loss was mine and only mine. For the others, it was just a matter of words.

Fathima madam pulled a chair and sat with me for a long time, with my hand in hers. Then she started sobbing. And just like that, I began to cry as well.

Fathima madam is one of the strictest managers in our office. I have never seen her be tender with anyone. We radio artistes tremble when we hear her name. If we are late in inserting ads or God forbid, miss an ad during the programme, she turns the office upside down. As far as she is concerned, the station exists to broadcast ads. News and other programmes are filler items.

What is more, our office has a strict rule banning any non-professional relationship between management and artistes. And now, without paying heed to any of this, she was sobbing loudly in front of me. So there I was, stuck, trying to comfort someone who had come to comfort me. When she finished crying, she opened her bag and showed me a strip of pills.

'This is what keeps me alive these days, Sameera. Some day, without this, I might die,' she said, her face red. I had no idea what was wrong with her. Did she have some mental illness? She understood my confusion.

'Sameera, all this happened when you were away. One day when I left the station, a taxi started following my car. It was parked right outside our main gates, as if waiting for me. The driver tracked me closely, always keeping two or three cars between us. I didn't think it was a big deal at first. But after the taxi missed a couple of opportunities to overtake me, I noticed it and was struck by a lightning bolt of suspicion. When I saw that the taxi was still behind me after I stopped at a bakery and then at a cafeteria to buy sandwiches for my children, I couldn't ignore it any more. Just to make sure I was not being paranoid, I went out of my way into a couple of galis. I took a U-turn at a signal and drove back the way I had just come and then went around a roundabout and got back on my route. The taxi was still behind me. I started sweating. My legs were trembling. I pressed down on the accelerator. The taxi speeded to keep up with me. I slowed down and so did the taxi. I cut through two red lights to escape. But the taxi followed me through the red lights. It followed me all the way home.

'When I got out of the car to open the garage, an

enormous man got out of that taxi and approached me. That's the last thing I remember. When I opened my eyes, I was lying in bed. Syed's mother and sisters were sitting by my bedside. They told me that some passers-by had found me lying unconscious on the street, and brought me home. I have never been so scared in my life, Sameera.

'I saw that taxi driver again and again. On the street, in the bazaar, at the park. And many other places. Wherever I look, he is there. Sometimes just beyond the window, sometimes on the roof of the opposite building. I hear the doorbell ring and run to look through the peephole and he is in the corridor. Or I hear a movement in the bathroom and when I check, he is hiding behind the door. When I walk on the streets, I can hear his careful footsteps. In the supermarket, I can see his shadow looming two aisles away.

'I told myself it was my imagination but I didn't believe myself. I didn't know what was real any more – the reality of my mind or the reality in which everyone else lived. My fears reached the point where my baba took me to a psychologist. When I take the pills the doctor has given me, I feel better. And that is how I am surviving now. Not just me. My father, mother and even my son, who is in the fifth standard, we are all on these pills now. You know Sameera, it was on the third day after that man followed me home, that Syed went missing . . .'

Fathima madam went back to her seat, her breath heavy with exhaustion. I continued to sit there, numb, not knowing what to say or think.

Javed, that was the day I got your letter.

A Place Not My Own

Our studio airs two different FM stations at two different frequencies. Orange Radio, which operates at 103.6, is the Hindi station, and Tunes Malayalam, which operates at 98.7, is the Malayalam station. The government had auctioned off the two frequencies to Broadway Communications, our parent company. After Arabic, Hindi and Malayalam are the most widely spoken languages in this city. Both our stations share one live studio, so we alternate with each other. When the Hindi team is live, the Malayalam team airs a recorded news programme, and vice versa. Of course listeners never figured out all these logistical arrangements. In fact, it took me a while after I joined to understand how it all worked.

We had no rivals in the city, so we competed against each other. If Tunes planned a new music programme, we would come up with a live game show. If they declared a prize, we would try to declare a bigger gift voucher. We argued endlessly about our ratings. We claimed more listeners and they claimed more advertisers. And maybe because of that, Rajeevan sir and the rest of the management were a bit biased towards them. That made the Tunes staff swagger a little. They did have a good team. Sharon, Minesh Menon, Viju Prasad, Anamika, Sheetal, Mridula, Ashwathi Pillai. Viju Prasad and Sheetal were the news people, the others were in entertainment. We called them the 'Malayalam Mafia', usually behind their backs, but when annoyed, to their face too.

15

Imthiaz sir, Charuhasan sir, Shahbaz, Sumayya Naseer, Meera Maskan – we were the Orange team. Meera ran a couple of live programmes and read the morning and evening news. Besides regulars like us, there were also a few part-time guest artistes.

Since the broadcast centre was affiliated to the Ministry of Information, there were several other stations in several languages running out of the centre, including BBC at 101.9. Though we were all different stations, since the studio and the technical facilities belonged to the government, it might be best to describe us as several small outfits, operating under one umbrella. Like many stores in one mall.

You know how it is when you arrive in a new place and feel like you don't belong there? That hesitation to reckon with a new geography. That knowledge that this place is not mine, these ways of talking are not mine, these silences are not mine, this etiquette is not mine. So many new things to absorb. And the place also takes a little time to accept the new person. Often you have to meet the place on its own terms. Sometimes you have to work hard to earn your little corner in it. Till that place becomes yours, till you find your own equilibrium there, there will be a gap between you and the place.

It was at the studio that I first experienced this. It seemed a very strange place to me in the beginning. Till I arrived in the City, India was something I had feared. I had always seen Indians as my enemies. Enemies who were lying in wait to attack my village, my Lahore, my Faisalabad, my Peshawar. They were shooting into my borders, making terrorists out of the poor fishermen they captured, branding poor wood

16

collectors in the border forests as trespassers and killing them. They were lining up my innocent brothers and sisters in Kashmir, shooting them point blank and publishing their photos in newspapers, labelling them terrorists. Each and every Indian terrified me. On my first day in the studio, I was shocked to see all the Indians walking around. How would I work among so many monsters? Impossible! What if they all turned against me and killed me?

I puzzled over my dilemma all evening. This was a job I had longed for, and I had fought for it at home. I was embarrassed to admit that I did not want it any longer. Even more embarrassed to admit that I no longer wanted it because of all the Indians in the office. I knew what baba would say, 'Then don't go any more.' I wanted to go and I didn't want to go.

I made up some pretext to go to mamu's house that night. First, mamu teased me. But when he saw that I was serious, he reasoned with me.

'Sameera, that's the kind of silly notion we hold on to when in our little country. Once you step out, you realize there are good people and bad people all over the world. National boundaries are just illusions. And okay, so what if they are these monsters you make them out to be? Then your job is to face them with courage. You have Khan blood in you. The Khans have never failed in a fight. Go win the fight. God knows your tongue is strong enough . . .'

If mamu hadn't cheered me up that day, I would have quit my job on day one. But in fact, much faster than I expected, I began to belong in the studio. I started looking forward to every day and every moment I spent there.

17

In all these days, I have never taken an unnecessary day off from work. While everyone else waited for the weekend, I waited for the beginning of the week. If someone was on holiday, I leaped at the opportunity to do their show, whereas my co-workers groaned at the burden. Nobody wanted to do the 10 p.m. live show, Pillow Music. Except me.

'At this rate, baji will have to move into the studio,' Nawaaz would say. 'Tell us the truth, baji, do you have a secret lover at the studio?' Farhana teased me. That's how crazy I was about the studio.

But now – I have lost all that excitement about going to the studio. My heart turns to stone when I step outside the house in the morning soon after the driver's missed call.

Cattle Class Mercedes

Our office vehicle is a Toyota minibus that can seat sixteen people. We call it 'Cattle Class Mercedes'. There can be no better name for this vehicle. It is practically a bullock cart. Although it looks good from the outside, the inside is a different story. The air conditioning doesn't work unless it is a good day for your zodiac. But astrology or not, it is out of commission for a couple of days every week.

Yunus, our driver, was a sweet man. 'Madam, it's a new vehicle. But the engine seems to be acting up . . .' He always had excuses.

Yunus would give me a missed call from the street outside my house at sharp six-fifty in the morning so that I could get in for the live show at eight. He would wait for a minute more and give me another missed call. If I didn't get into the car by then, he would leave. I couldn't blame him. By the time he did the rounds of hundreds of streets and gave missed calls to all the RJs and survived the traffic jams and waited at every signal in the city at least twice over, it would often be past eight. Kapil bhai or Asif bhai, whoever was at the switchboard, would cover for us with a song or an ad till we ran in and got on air. Being yelled at by Imthiaz sir had become a daily ritual.

Then we did it all over again in the afternoon. By the time I got home after the morning show and touring the city, it would be four or five. I would get dropped off at the very end, being the furthest along the route, with only one other person remaining, a Sri Lankan man who worked in IT. Several times I had proposed, very reasonably, that since I was the first to get picked up, I should be the first to get dropped off. But the Malayalam Mafia stood as one against my appeal. Once or twice a month, as a favour, they would let me get dropped off first. But in return, I had to buy them juice or samosas along the way.

Around the time I had joined, Cattle Class was completely dominated by the Malayalam Mafia. As soon as I got into the minibus, I could hear their annoying chatter, their voices like stones in a tin can. They were experts in speaking exclusively in Malayalam, without using even a single word from Hindi or English, so that the rest of us might not even guess what they were saying. Later they even started a radio programme based on this. I would plead with them, 'Aren't you tired of blabbing in your own language all day? Why not give it a rest now?' And they would retort, 'That was for the public, this is just for us.'

We had a staff member from Morocco who complained that the Malayalam Mafia was talking about him constantly. Eventually that made him quit the job. This was how the Malayalam Mafia operated, I realized later, when they wanted to smoke out someone they didn't like. They had sent three others packing since my arrival, but their pranks did not work on me.

Also in the bus were two Filipinas, Joanna and Irene, who worked on the admin side. The Malayalam Mafia referred to them as Sasikala and Pushpalatha. The women had no idea. As soon as Irene and Joanna got on the bus, they would put on their headphones and lose themselves in music. After that, even if the Malayalam Mafia turned the bus upside down, they wouldn't care.

Whereas I couldn't just sit and listen to music amidst all that cacophony. My ears would tune into the conversations, even without my knowledge. At first I tried reasoning with them that all Cattle Class conversations should take place in a common language and that I too had a right to enjoy their jokes. But the Malayalam Mafia did not listen to me. Once in a while when they broke off to speak in Hindi or English, they would sneak in some taunts, aimed deliberately at me and Shahbaz. Hot-headed Shahbaz wouldn't let it slide. He would lash back, completely out of proportion, and Hasan, our translator, would join him. Then it would become a free for all. At first I simply listened to these quarrels but slowly I joined the Shahbaz–Hasan faction. Not so much because

I agreed with them, but because I wanted to disagree with the Malayalam Mafia.

Maybe Pakistan had lost a match to India that day, or maybe our border forces had fired some shots into the air, or maybe one of the two countries had sent up a missile. Or there was a terrorist attack somewhere in India. Or one of the foreign ministers had made a controversial statement. I had to take responsibility for whatever it was. You know me, Javed. Would I take something like that lying down? Each day's travels in Cattle Class would end in our own war. Some days I would try to ignore them. But you know how some kids will stick their hands down a dog's throat so they can get themselves bitten? The Malayalam Mafia was like that. They would drop some controversial topic into the conversation to get a rise out of me. Viju Prasad, news coordinator of the Malayalam department, was especially good at this. Ya Allah, he was something else. He was convinced that India was the most amazing country in the whole world. India had invented rockets, airplanes, the Internet, mobile phones, test tube babies! Poor Shahbaz and Hasan would gape numbly as he boasted. But not me. I know my history. I did not have to listen open-mouthed to this crap.

The most annoying of Viju Prasad's many brags was that India was the only country that had never attacked any other country in the last five thousand years. At first, I pretended I didn't hear this. Then one day, I got back at him. 'Yes, it's true that India has not invaded anyone in the last five thousand years. You know why?' I asked. 'Because India didn't have

21

the time. You Indians are too busy attacking other Indians. Kill everyone inside before killing those outside, that is your clever strategy.' That shut him up. Grudgingly they acknowledged that I could hold my own. Those days were such fun, with our silly arguments and debates. The hours in the car passed so quickly.

But yesterday when I got into the bus after the show, Cattle Class felt melancholic. The happy, heated conversations had subsided. The arguments and counterarguments were gone. Everyone was silent. Instead of Yunus, there was a new driver. Apparently one day Yunus had quarrelled with someone and simply walked out, never to return. No one knows where he is. The front seat, where Hasan used to sit and support me in my battle against the Malayalam Mafia, lay vacant. Shahbaz lost his zest for life. Joanna had taken leave and left the country during the revolution and she did not return. And without anyone to fight them, the Malayalam Mafia too lost its gusto. They spoke in soft voices, perhaps out of sympathy for me, perhaps in mourning for Hasan, perhaps worried about Yunus. Or maybe they were wondering about their own place in this country. Javed, the City has lost its happy face. Today it is a city of fear.

Island

During the busy workday at the studio, I forgot everything. But when I returned, the empty room was there to remind me. Memories, like honeybees, buzzed around me. Images came racing out of the corners of my mind, even though

I tried hard to forget them. Baba lying on the sofa and watching TV. My tea waiting for me in its cup, with a lid on top. Dinner for the night, cooked and ready. I remembered all those times that I had offered to make tea or cook dinner, and how every single time baba had refused. Doing it by himself had brought him a profound happiness. Baba had lived alone in this city for twenty-two long years. A life of aloneness – of coming home alone after work, of cooking dinner alone, of washing clothes alone, of ironing them alone, of making his bed alone. Bade taya had invited him several times to come and stay with the family but baba refused. He had also not got a visa to bring us over. He must have realized soon enough that it was impossible to support a family on his income in this big city. And by the time he was able to afford it, he had got used to this solitary life. When I joined him, he was planning to continue in a rented flat, but my uncles and aunts opposed the plan, insisting that it was not a good idea to leave a young girl by herself at home all day. And so baba finally acquiesced and we moved into Taya Ghar.

I wondered then where my life was taking me. I felt anxious about living side by side with the chachas, mamus and mamis I only knew from their occasional visits home. It was my first time living away from ma. I knew better than to expect the kind of love and affection ma had given me.

Taya Ghar is a big house, which taya had divided into several flats. There are six families here, with fourteen children among them. One of the flats is shared by four single men who are related to us. The downstairs kitchen and the living-cum-dining area are common spaces. Three families including bade taya's and chhote taya's families live downstairs. And three families including baba and me and two other chachas live upstairs. There is a small kitchen up here in case the upstairs families want to make some coffee or a few chapattis for dinner. Everyone comes together at mealtimes or when guests visit. Otherwise we all stick to our little corners of this house. And so, though we seem like a joint family, we all manage to safeguard our privacy. This was bade taya's dream too: a family house where all the brothers could live together even in this foreign city, while leading their own private lives. It was he who searched for a suitable house and renovated it to make separate flats. And perhaps that is why, among our friends and family, the house came to be named after him.

A small sitting area, a bedroom, and a bathroom. This was the small universe that baba and I had carved out for ourselves in Taya Ghar. Even though it was tiny, I loved it from the start. The bedroom had a small balcony that faced a highway. I learned later that others in the house had rejected the room because of the roadside noise. But that did not trouble me. I could sit in the balcony and stare at the sky for as long as I wanted, gazing at birds and airplanes. Below was the road with vehicles and people in them. And far away was the skyline with its big buildings and glittering lights.

Just beyond the highway was a small park that got busy in the evenings, with crowds of people on its green bed of grass. People came to walk, to let their kids play, to swing on the swings, to enjoy a round of badminton or a game of football. Young men came to show off, couples came to sit and talk. A bit later, there would be picnicking families, and I would watch their little arguments and love stories. That balcony was a window to a wide world and that flat was the home of my dreams.

Baba gave me the bedroom and started sleeping in a small cot in the front room. Other than when he needed to change clothes or iron them, he never came to the bedroom. His space was now in the living room, in front of the TV.

To be honest, in the beginning, life in the house was boring. Imagine a father and daughter who did not really have much of a relationship, alone with each other in a flat. We had nothing to talk about at first. The twenty years that baba had lived alone in this city had created a distance between us. And baba had always been frugal in conversation. That frugality only increased when his adult daughter came to stay. Our flat felt like a quiet, stern military camp. We breathed freely only when we joined the rest of Taya Ghar at mealtimes or when we visited the other flats. But I did not let baba continue with his grave ways. Within six months, I charmed him. Baba started melting before my eyes. He began speaking openly and laughing freely.

Today when I walked into the flat, I remembered a childhood story of mine that baba had recounted to me. I was six or seven years old and losing my milk teeth. I was afraid of having my teeth plucked. One of my relatives tried to get rid of my fears by telling me that my tooth would turn into gold if I left it inside a book. I asked baba if that was true. Baba said yes, hoping that would encourage me. But I had more questions – how long should I keep the tooth in the book, how much gold per tooth, would I get more gold if I left it in the book for longer? After baba gave reassuring replies to all my questions, I asked him to give me two of his teeth so that I could turn them into gold . . .

Baba laughed a lot that day, remembering my precocious answer and I joined in, with some chagrin. Remembering that made me cry today, Javed. I missed baba all the more. I am only beginning to understand what I have lost. Everyone here thinks I am a very brave girl. What they don't know is that my laughter and confidence and all the noise I make is just a disguise. Deep inside, I am in pain and I don't want anyone to know. Even so, when I feel lonely, I try to call a friend. But everyone is busy. No one has the time to talk. This house is full of people but I am like an island in the middle.

Javed, why did fate isolate me like this? Why were the two people I loved taken away from me, beckoned into the depths of tragedy? Is life a series of questions without answers?

Harami

Ashraf aka bade taya has the final word in our family. He is baba's eldest brother. When he decides something, whether it's right or wrong, there are no appeals against it. This is not because of any authoritarian tendency of his, but from the deep respect he has earned from taking care of his family and fulfilling his responsibilities. It was taya who brought all the young men in his family above the age of twenty to this country. He got them jobs and married them off well. He took on dada's responsibilities and fulfilled them even more meticulously than dada would have. And the family hasn't forgotten that. Baba and his other brothers do not even sit in front of him or raise their voices when he is near. They never go against a decision he takes. If anyone fears him a little less, it is us, the younger generation.

Taya first came here with the help of a distant uncle of his. He spent a long time searching for a job, applying to many firms. None of them gave him work, and some told him that he was not qualified to even be a helper. In those days, another uncle of taya's had a barber shop in the souk, which dated back to the fifties when the British had ruled. In those days, all the important men of the city came to that shop to get shaves and haircuts. Taya used to go and sit there with a long face. One day a senior police officer went there for a haircut when taya was around. He remembered taya from his last visit too, and asked the uncle about this young man sitting in the barber shop. Mamu humbly informed him that this was his unemployed nephew. The police officer told taya to come to the police headquarters the next day. Taya went and was hired as an office boy. Over many years of hard work, rising through the ranks, taya made it to the position of civil sergeant. He taught himself Arabic, mathematics, computers, emailing. He learned to google. An Englishman would be impressed if he heard taya speak English today. And without anyone's help, he is now a senior policeman.

He was also responsible for my arrival in the City. By the time baba began dreaming of it, taya had planned for it. I boarded a plane to get here before I even got my degree certificates in hand. This human trafficking was the result of my mother's tearful phone calls full of fears about losing control over me if I continued to live in the village. I did not want to come. I even complained to my mother that it would have been better if she'd married me off to some Taliban guy. What kind of work would I get without even a certificate? I was sitting in Taya Ghar pitying myself when the programme coordinator of Orange Radio, Imthiaz sir, happened to tell Anwar mamu that he was looking for a young woman who could handle the Hindi programme. They were old friends. 'I do know a chatterbox girl. But her Urdu is stronger than her Hindi,' mamu said. 'Oh, we have lots of Urdu listeners as well,' Imthiaz sir replied. It would be ideal if she could mix both. Anyhow, bring her in for an interview.'

When Anwar mamu told me this the next day, I exploded with happiness. I had longed for such a job.

'I would do this job even for no pay,' I exclaimed.

'But do you know Hindi?' Anwar mamu asked.

'Anyone who knows how to use their tongue can speak Hindi. Don't worry,' I assured him.

I had learned Urdu and Farsi in school, not Hindi. And I had picked up a little Arabic, as my third language. My knowledge of Hindi came entirely from Bollywood movies. Thanks to the Khans of Bollywood, I could manage a little Hindi. I decided that was enough to try my hand at the job.

But everyone at home was against my working in radio. Sippy auntie led the opposition with baba and all my chachas and mamus siding with her. They argued that the radio job was all about flirting with men. And the women in the house agreed with them. When it seemed that everyone had

28

abandoned me, one person alone came forward to support me. My bade taya, Sergeant Ashraf Amjad Khan!

'You all may live in this city but you might as well be in Faisalabad for all you know of the world. This is a different city. If a girl gets to become a radio jockey here, it is a matter of pride, not embarrassment. Our Sameera has a gift for talking. Why should we waste an opportunity she has to express herself?' Taya asked, looking directly at Sippy auntie.

'It's true. And after all, it's not forever, just till her certificates arrive and she can look for a job. Why should she sit at home and be bored till then?' When Aisha auntie also unexpectedly came on board for me, the men stopped wagging their tongues.

And on the day of my interview, it was my taya who came with me, taking baba's place as my guardian. He did not want me to lose this job for lack of a supportive presence. That's taya for you.

I was interviewed by the managing director Rajeevan sir as well as Imthiaz sir and Fathima madam. They asked me to do a commentary for an India–Pakistan cricket match, a mock live-in with Fathima madam, interview Rajeevan sir about his job as managing director, and sing a Hindi song. At the end of the interview, Rajeevan sir asked me when I could join.

'Sahib, even without your recommendation, this Sameera would have become a radio jockey. She's such a smart talker. I have no doubt that she's going to be a star,' Imthiaz sir patted my shoulder when we were leaving.

Everyone at home was wondering why taya, who had a

29

reputation for his honesty and impartiality, for not bowing his head to ask for favours, had set out to help me get this ordinary radio job. Some said it was because of a special fondness for me as the first girl-child of my generation and others thought it might be out of a special regard for baba. But I knew of yet another secret reason. My fierce taya who could easily take on the entire world feared only one person on earth and that was his wife, my Sippy auntie. (Her real name was Zulfi, but long ago some toddler in the family had anointed her Sippy with his unformed tongue and the name stuck. She herself preferred it.)

The unwritten law of Taya Ghar was that nothing happened without Sippy auntie's approval. Even taya was not exempt. But you know me a little, don't you? You think I would go along with that? By the age of twelve I had learnt to return ma's fierce glances and respond with twelve words for every word she spoke. By the time I was in college, I had learned to ignore her scolding and retreat into my room with my cellphone. Remember how you guys used to call me, secretly and not-so-secretly, a harami chhokri? That was me, not just outside but also inside the house. I did not waste too much obedience on my dada and dadi, or chachas, mamus and mamis. I can even say proudly that my family grudgingly learnt to respect me for expressing my opinions to anyone's face, for charming my way into getting what I wanted. My biggest admirer was taya. And the main reason for that was that even in the brief interludes during which they came for their holidays, I was able to best Sippy auntie. Taya secretly enjoyed my performances.

And so whenever I put forward my point of view, taya would concede that I had a point. 'He who knows Farsi is obviously educated,' he would preface his support of me.

The women of the household often used me as the middlewoman when they wanted favours from the men. Like a persuasive insurance agent, I became good at getting my stern and practical uncles to do what I wanted. And that was taya's idea: I would be the mediator between him and Sippy auntie; he used me when he wanted to get Sippy auntie to agree to something. The funny thing is, Sippy auntie also used me exactly like this. Though she ruled the house, Sippy auntie was scared of taya and never did anything without his permission. He never knew though. They were both afraid of each other and used me and that strong, bold tongue of mine for getting their work done.

Taya Ghar

On weekends and holidays Taya Ghar was crowded with guests. Most of them came to seek favours from taya or complain to him. A job for someone, a land dispute back in the village, suspicion about a wife . . . they were convinced that taya had all the solutions. Like a zamindar, taya would sit in a chair in the middle and listen. He would get them jobs in small companies here and there or call a politician in the village to solve disputes. And so everyone in the city had faith in him. They believed that Ashraf sahib's Taya Ghar was a place of solutions.

Besides strangers, there would also be distant uncles, cousins and young bachelors who knew the family from back home. At least twenty people sat down to eat lunch, after Jum'a prayers. Taya insisted on feeding everyone who came home on that day.

That was also the day all the women worked together in the kitchen. During the week, each woman made meals for her own family. But on holidays, we all joined together to make a biriyani. Or rice and mutton masala curry.

Though the other men would not even come to the kitchen door, baba and Khalid chacha would work with us in the kitchen, if they were around in the house. Baba's mutton masala was famous in the city. When he used to live alone, friends and family requested him to come and visit, and bring along his mutton masala. And baba enjoyed spending time in the kitchen, where the news of the week and all the gossip got freely shared.

There were some regular guests who contributed to the kitchen life. One such was Baluchi Barber who would arrive at nine in the morning.

I don't know why that uncle was called Baluchi, and if that was his real name. From the time I'd known him, he was called Baluchi. No one knew him by a different name. Baluchi Barber's arrival would transform taya into a real zamindar – taya would stretch his legs and sit in the living room, like in the old black-and-white movies. Baluchi Barber would trim taya's moustache, shave his face, cut his hair and keep murmuring in his ear. Then Baluchi Barber would come to the kitchen. Sitting at the threshold, he would tell us everything that had happened in the city, including who had just arrived from the village, whose daughter was getting married, who had just lost their job and who was about to leave on umra.

Another regular was Chamar chacha, a cobbler who would come every week to the gali in front of Taya Ghar. Perhaps he was the last surviving cobbler in the City. He had come here long ago, from some village near Lahore, and continued to ply the same trade. He had at the most two or three customers a day. I always puzzled over how Chamar chacha with his small job and tiny income survived in this big, expensive city. What could he save from his meagre income? What would he send home to his village? And how would they survive on that? Thinking about this made me sad. And so once a month at least, I would take him my shoes, even though they were in good condition. 'Beti, these shoes have all their stitches, what do you need me to do?' he would ask, turning the shoes around in his hands. 'No chacha, nothing is broken, just reinforce it,' I would tell him.

By lunchtime, Chamar chacha would also come to Taya Ghar. Taya had many acquaintances like Chamar chacha. 'When I was wandering around jobless, he brought me something to drink. I must not forget them in my good days,' taya would say. There were a couple of them that I especially liked. One was Amir chacha. Baba would say laughingly, he has a loose nut somewhere in there. Amir chacha would bring with him interesting gossip from the city. He also knew how to tell a story. And so as soon as chacha arrived, all the womenfolk would gather around the table to hear his stories.

Another guest I loved was Karim chacha, but for completely different reasons. While all the men I knew, including my own baba, were constantly worrying about raising their daughters, Karim chacha was delighted to have four daughters. Occasionally he could be heard complaining to Allah for not giving him more daughters. He did not distinguish between his two sons and his four daughters, loving and respecting and educating them in equal measure.

I have visited his home back in the village. It is a joy to be a woman in that house. Karim chacha had painstakingly created such a home. I have often felt that he was madder than a drunk Sufi. His ideas about love and women were too radical for ordinary men.

According to his philosophy, a household without girls was like a tree without flowers. And the more the flowers, the prettier the tree. Smiling gently, he would say, 'When my beautiful daughters grow up, young men will circle the house like honeybees, eager for a taste of nectar. I'll be a proud father then. It won't be too long now before lines of young men will form outside my door, each begging my permission to marry my daughter. But they will all be disappointed. I want to see them wandering through the streets, sick with love, muttering the names of my daughters, like Punnu in the tale of Sassi Punnu. A woman must fall in love on her own. The devil will find a home in the heart of a woman who does not fall in love. She will wreck her home. Whereas love turns women into angels. In the matter of love, a woman should be as wise as a snake and as sharp-eyed as an eagle. Only a stupid woman would fall in love with the first good-looking man she meets. She should not surrender to just anyone.'

Karim chacha's advice to every woman was to wait till she found the man that Allah had chosen for her. But how to find him? I often heard him advising his young daughters, 'You must watch him secretly. Keep an eye on his actions and words. The sign of a good lover is not how much he loves you. And in fact if he loves you too much, be careful. Maybe he is selfish. There is no greater misery than living with a selfish man or a suspicious one. On the other hand, you can trust him fully if he respects the Prophet, reads books, bears himself with dignity, speaks with humility, respects women, treats poor people kindly, loves children and is optimistic about life. If you find such a man, whoever he is, I will marry you to him. And I will respect your womanly ability to find such a man.'

He didn't merely dream dreams and spout advice – when his oldest daughter found a man who fit this description, he approved wholeheartedly and got them married. 'I don't have wealth or status or a big house. I only have one thing to be proud of: I am the father of four daughters,' Karim chacha would often say, earning my admiration.

Farhana

Yesterday I went for a walk in the souk by myself. I was feeling suffocated in the room. Taya and mamu wouldn't approve if they knew, but I needed to get out at least a little bit.

When I got ready and went downstairs, Farhana was sitting in the hall. 'Baji, where are you going?' she asked.

'Going to the souk for a walk.'

'Want me to come with you?'

'No, I don't need any company,' I said, stepping outside.

My mamus' and chachas' children are mostly boys, and there are thirteen of them. All of them are high-voltage characters – imagine sulphuric acid with arms and legs. The oldest of them, Nawaaz, is only seventeen years old and the youngest is three. By rights, they are all kissing cousins of mine and I would often tease them, 'Couldn't you kids have been born a little earlier? Then we could have held hands and fallen in love. Instead, now I have you trailing me everywhere calling me baji, baji.' I am fond of them all. The only girl among my cousins is Farhana, Ahlaq chacha's daughter. She is in eleventh standard in one of the Pakistani schools in the city. You know what they say about Sahiba, the heroine of our folk love stories, 'Nine angels died the moment they saw how beautiful she was.' That could be about Farhana. She was that kind of beautiful.

We have been friends since when she used to come to the village for the holidays. And after I moved here, our friendship deepened. She would tell me about every little thing going on in her life. She was seeing a boy. A Punjabi boy studying in the twelfth standard in the Indian school. She showed me his photo on her cellphone. Handsome guy. But this sardarji of hers struck me as old-fashioned, wearing his turban even in these modern times. I don't know where she found the courage to fall in love with him. People say this is a practical age, that kids these days don't fall in love

36

till they check religion, caste, race and colour. But I think that is just how adults like to comfort themselves. Young people have never checked off lists before they fall in love – they love whom they love. Like Farhana with her Pravin Kumar. They met at the bus stop. Sometimes she shows me their messages. XXX-rated messages that make even me go, 'What!'

At home Farhana is quiet; she has had a strict upbringing. Her baba and her ma are always around her. Yet she coolly manages to deceive them. I once asked her, 'Farhana, won't you get into trouble if chacha or chachi saw these messages?'

'Baji, you are so silly. You think I haven't thought through this? I have saved his number as "Lulu Centre". If a message comes when I am with baba or ma, I go, "Oh these shopping promotions. What a pain they are." I'll even open the message and read it aloud. "Hurry, hurry, up to 50 per cent reduction on every item for the next three days . . . Come and enjoy."'

I laughed thinking of Farhana's little game. Poor chacha and chachi, who don't know any English; they had to believe her. Instead of going to school, Farhana would roam around shopping malls and go to the movies with him. 'But if you are wearing your school uniform, won't people know you should be in school?' I thought I was asking a legitimate question. 'I think you have lost all your common sense by hanging out with the idiot Indians in your studio,' she said in exasperation. 'After all, I learned all these tricks from seeing you trick mama when I came to visit you on vacations. And now you are asking me this. Baji, how hard is it to avoid school uniform? Who would doubt me if I say today is a special day at school, Earth Day, Green Day, Mother's Day, Labour Day . . .' I had to bow before her cunning. I am sure I didn't play as many tricks on my baba.

By mistake, I asked her one day, 'My child, when did you become old enough to fall in love?' 'What to do, baji. I told myself, wait for a couple of years before starting all this. But this body, fed on animal meat and muscle, does this body listen to me? After all, only the body knows what it wants. One of these days, I think I might just attack him and ravage him on the street.' That was her response. I am scared to ask her whether she has actually done something with him. She might just say yes.

If I went on a walk with her, she would talk non-stop about her exploits. Not for a minute can she be silent. Today I want to walk alone. All by myself.

A City Without a Name

I walked alone for a long time, through narrow streets and interlacing alleys that were centuries old. They were all mostly empty. And the few people I passed by walked in a hurry, as if they were afraid of someone. They looked fearfully at parked cars. Perhaps they wondered if any of them would explode. Or maybe they were afraid a gunman would appear suddenly out of a hidden corner and shoot everyone on the street before disappearing. That was the kind of news we were hearing about the neighbouring countries. Who could be sure that wouldn't happen in this country as well.

Javed, the only reason I am not naming these streets is because their names are unimaginative. It is enough to call this place 'City'. The rulers of this place have built a bunch of roads in their own names, cheapening their country's name even further. This used to be the city of the Sumerians, who, three thousand years before Christ, worshipped a mother goddess called Enki. After that, Achaemenids, Parthians and Sassanids ruled the City in turn. After the onset of Islam, Persian emperors, Caliphs and the Ottomans walked the City. Then the Portuguese took over and after them, the British. When they left, the Caliphs returned. But still, the name of this city does not play on our heartstrings the way Baghdad, Cairo, Basra, Tehran, Damascus, Faisalabad, Istanbul, and Hyderabad do. I don't know why.

These streets have been trading with India and Pakistan for hundreds of years. It was the Gujarati banias who brought the world to this city. They brought clothes from Bombay, tin lamps from Cairo, carpets from Persia and Turkish Delight from Istanbul. They were the ones who transformed an abandoned city into a city of celebrations. I still remember how vibrant and happy these streets were when I first arrived. The Malabari Gali, where Indian clothes were sold, was always crowded. The shops that sold Kashmiri shawls and cotton churidar kurtas from Pakistan were full of plump Gujarati women. The gossipy merchants seated in front of their shops selling Persian carpets, the vendors who came out of their Made in Malaysia electronics stores to lead customers in by hand, the Bangladeshi men hawking cheap Chinese trinkets, the money exchange dadas waiting for foreigners in front of heaps of currency notes, the men playing dice at the side of the road and talking to the parrots in their cages . . . my favourite were the shops selling sweets and spices. I would wander near them just to enjoy the fragrance of cardamom, cinnamon, ginger, cumin and pepper. The vendors called me beti and offered me almonds, pistachios, cashew nuts, dried figs and watermelon seeds. They all used to know baba and he had introduced me to them proudly. 'This is my daughter. Very educated. She works for the radio . . .'

Those were happy days. But like a river that freezes suddenly in mid-flow, all those happinesses have disappeared.

Most of the shops are now half-shuttered, and shopkeepers live in constant fear. How quickly this city where people trusted each other turned into a city of hostilities. Where there was once friendship, there is now suspicion.

I had turned to go home when an Arab woman coming from the opposite direction surprised me by suddenly reaching out and holding my hand.

'Do you recognize me?' Her voice was heavy with gloom.

I shook my head after searching my memory for her face.

'We met once before. I am your friend Ali's mother.'

'Ali? Ali Fardan?'

'Yes, that Ali.'

'I remember, yes, I remember,' I said, my voice trembling. 'We used to travel together.'

'He used to talk about you a lot. He was fond of you.' She embraced me and started crying.

Her tears burned my face. I could not stand there, my face touching hers. Freeing myself, I ran, like a wild animal, through galis full of shadows.

Part 2

Second Class

Lahore Gali

You think I am being mysterious, Javed. But I am not. I am afraid that if I open the door to my memory, I might suck you into the narrow air shafts of my life. Who has the time to listen to other people's tragedies? But since you insist, I will tell you the whole story. Let me reassure you though, that the story does not end unhappily. Or maybe I prefer to believe that, even at times like this when nothing can be guaranteed. I believe that you create your own future through your thoughts. Humans don't walk towards dreams, dreams come to us. I try to think good thoughts and dream good dreams. I look at the future with hope. And so I feel confident that tomorrow will be better.

Ali Fardan was a good friend of Hasan, our Arabic translator and fellow Cattle Class passenger. He was one of the technical staff at the radio station. If we had any technical problems, he, along with his assistant Muneer Gazi, would look into it. Even if there were no technical problems, both of them could be seen wandering around the studio, screwdrivers in hand, in the name of 'maintenance'. Ali would stop to chat with everyone, especially young women.

At first, the Malayalam Mafia tricked me into thinking that their names were Ali Nair and Muneer Choudhry. Like an idiot, I believed them. They also called Waleed Rahman, in our accounts department, Waleed Pillai. They had many jokes like that.

Ali spoke a hybrid language that mixed Arabic, Hindi and English. He had also picked up a few Malayalam words by befriending the Malayalam Mafia. It was fun to hear him talk, and Sumayya and Meera Maskan would often stop him for a chat just to listen to him.

Till about a year ago, my only interaction with Ali in the twenty-eight months I had worked at the studio, was an occasional hello at the canteen or near the restrooms. But then one day there was a huge debate at lunchtime in our canteen about the most beautiful game in the world. The Malayalam Mafia was on one side and on the other was Ali, Hasan, and Ahmed from Hit Arabia. Naturally, according to the Malayalam Mafia, the most beautiful game in the world was cricket, while Ali and gang argued that it was football. Both factions put forward their arguments. Usually I had no interest in participating in these quarrels on top of the everyday wrestling matches in Cattle Class. But that day I couldn't stand the Malayalam Mafia winning the debate. Though I secretly agreed with them, I joined the Ali faction. I said that cricket is a one-man show and it is the man of the match who usually wins the game. But in football, you can see the beauty of teamwork. And finally, I argued, the pleasure of winning as a team is much bigger than the pleasure of winning for oneself. Even I was impressed with my glowing performance.

Ali expressed his gratitude by asking me for my Facebook name. I couldn't say no. He sent me a thank you message and a friend request. I accepted and added him to my friends list. The next day, he invited me to be the postmaster of his 'Shia Village', an imaginary place in a Facebook game called City Villa. I accepted and invited him to be a police officer in my village, 'Lahore Gali'. Thus, two City Villa freaks stopped being strangers in the same office. After that, every day he sent me at least two 'energy' gifts. In return I offered him stamps or caps. He visited Lahore Gali and helped me harvest carrots or deliver goods to the bakery. And I sent guests to his music shop and assisted him with collecting rent from his buildings. Till then, the two of us, with our different languages, cultures and religions, had nothing in common. But now we had a Facebook dream city to build together.

I soon migrated from City Villa to Galaxy Life, Pet City, Howzat Cricket and other games. Ali moved on to Top Eleven, Fifa Superstar, Social War, Army Attack. But by then our friendship had a strong foundation. Ali and I soon found something else to bond over, beyond office and Facebook. Can you guess what that is, Javed? The same magic that brought you and me together.

String Walkers

One day in between recordings, I was chatting with Ali on Facebook and asked him, 'Wts pgrm aftr duty hrs . . .? Facebooking . . .?!!!'

'Facebook? Not when you have office hours for that!' he responded. First afternoon nap. Then a couple of hours of football. And then some evenings, he said, he played guitar with a group.

Guitar! The moment I heard that, a pang of desire, asleep till then, suddenly woke up and came rushing through my nerves to the very tips of my fingers. That's the power of music, isn't it? It might lie dormant but it never quite leaves your soul. We might forget music, but music does not forget us. It waits under layers of consciousness, as if listening for a summons.

I stared at my screen for a while, surprised that I had had no idea about his interest in music. I had never seen him play any musical instrument at an office party or celebration.

Javed, do you remember our little trips? Even now, ma has no idea that all those times that I left home for 'extra classes' I was actually taking guitar classes, that the tuition fees were going to my guitar teacher. Though Saima and Sameer figured it out after a while, they were too scared of me to tell her. Even after three years of guitar classes, ma did not see the guitar in my room till I was getting ready to come here. Her eyes probably still remain wide open in shock. Poor ma. She must have been scared to think of her daughter spending all that time with that djinn. I don't think she would have been that surprised if she had found a man hiding in my room. I longed to bring the guitar with me when I came here. But I was scared of baba and taya. I didn't feel confident of ruling over them the way I had ruled over ma. When I ceded my room to Saima, I had only one thing to say to her: do not even dare to touch the guitar.

Javed, my friend, I am indebted to you in so many ways – for opening a door to the enchanting world of music, for introducing me to a talented teacher like Suhail master, for accompanying me on those secret evening trips, and then on my nineteenth birthday, for gifting me that guitar that I had longed for. Without music, without those delicate notes that emerged from those strings, my life would have been a lesser thing.

After Ali mentioned the guitar gang, I couldn't sit still. Where do you meet? And when? Who is in it? Are there women in the group? Can I join? I chased after him with a hundred questions, like a buzzing bee. Then it was Ali's turn to be surprised. After all, he too had no idea that I was passionate about music. But I was disappointed to hear his answers. His music group met on Mondays and Wednesdays and their meetings often went on till as late as eleven in the night. And you couldn't just walk in and join them. Only an expert guitarist could join and you had to prove yourself in front of everyone in the group.

I knew I would somehow pass that test. But how could I make it to those night meetings? It was not as if eleven was a late hour in this city. For many people, that's when their day begins. Sometimes when I went shopping with Sippy auntie or my chachis, it would be eleven when we returned. On the weekends, if we went to visit one of our uncles or if guests came over, we would sit talking till at least twelve. But notwithstanding all that, if I said that I wanted to go out in the night with men, there would be an explosion in Taya Ghar. Dear heart, just forget that dream, I told myself.

So, for some days, I stamped my dream down. But after hearing Ali describe the evenings, the songs they sang, the notes that someone had composed – I had no peace of mind. I wanted to run my fingers on those strings. I was besotted, as if by a secret lover. I was soon ready to pay any price and go to any extreme.

For days, I planned and plotted. But nothing occurred to me. When I told Ali, he offered to take me there and bring me back, if I was ready to go with him. That encouraged me some more. At least that solved the transportation problem. Now it was a matter of getting out of the house.

Perhaps I could say that I was going to mamu's house. But what if someone called there? Or maybe I could invent some evening live shows or office gatherings. I knew, however, that if baba or taya cross-questioned me, I would not be able to stand up to it. That's when I really understood how claustrophobic this den of men was. Back in the village, I would have just announced that there was a college event and I would be home late. Ma would not ask any questions. Rather, I would not give her an opportunity to ask.

Finally, I mentioned my dilemma to Aisha auntie. She was a favourite of mine. I could talk to her openly about anything. 'Don't even bother asking your baba,' she advised me. 'Then everyone would get involved in the discussion. Just take the matter directly to taya.'

After all, what could taya do if I told him that I enjoyed music, played the guitar and wanted to meet some friends for musical evenings? Would he chew me up? All right then, let's see what happens. The harami inside me decided to take up the challenge.

And so one Monday, after confirming with Ali, I bravely strode up to taya to ask him for permission. As soon as I saw taya, my courage dissolved. I feel disgusted with myself when I think of it now. What a coward I was! I told him that I wanted to go to a friend's birthday party in the evening. Taya was silent for a minute and then he asked, 'Have you told your baba?'

'No, she just told me of the party today. I tried calling baba but didn't get through.'

'And you really want to go?'

'Yes.'

'Who are you going with?'

'My friend will pick me up and drop me off.'

Even after that, taya didn't say yes. After thinking for a minute, he said that if I really insisted on going, I could, as long as I took Nawaaz or Farhana with me.

Now I was stuck between the devil and the deep sea. Nawaaz could not be trusted. He was chhote taya's spoilt little darling. No backbone whatsoever. He would betray me if things came to a head. Farhana was the opposite. While she wouldn't betray me, she would overdo it completely. At a couple of parties I had taken her to, even broad-minded as I am, I was a bit outraged by her interaction with some young men there. I was scared of taking Farhana to an unfamiliar gathering, but decided in the end to go with her. And when I asked her, she agreed.

And that's how I first went to a String Walkers session.

Dum Maro Dum

It was then that I realized what was missing from my life in the city.

The spot itself was intoxicating – it was the backyard of a Starbucks on the beach. Almond trees, soft lamps, a grass lawn and wooden benches. It was not a busy place. A couple of old men come to smoke the hookah. Some Westerners who spoke in soft voices. A few middle-aged readers who did not look up from their books. Only the weekends got busy. That's why the String Walkers had chosen to meet on Monday and Wednesday evenings.

By the time we arrived with Ali, everyone else was already there. Ali introduced me around the table. Ali's friend Nazar Quraishy who worked for Citibank, his girlfriend Farah, a mixed-race young man called Ifran (his father was Arab and his mother was Dutch), Salman Muhammad from Hit Arabia (I remembered him from our canteen), Roger from the Philippines and his cousin Sofia. A miniature world. Such a gathering was possible only in cities like this, where immigrants came from everywhere.

Within minutes, the group won me over. On each meeting, one member of the group was to begin playing a new number. The next person would riff off on what was played before. It was like an invisible contest. But each musician in the group also had his or her own style. Nazar played in the Persian tradition and knew all its famous songs. Roger and Salman played in various rock and roll bands and that was how they knew each other. Sofia would compete with them. Farah was more interested in classical music while Ifran loved Latin guitar, especially Samba. Ali was unsurpassed in Arabic music and the blues.

Since I was auditioning, there was no contest that day. Nazar and Roger played a couple of their favourite numbers. Then Ali asked me to play something. In fact, after seeing them perform, I felt a little uneasy. After all, I had not trained in any style to speak of. But I desperately wanted to be one of them, and so, hoping against hope, I played a remixed version of that old song, the one that had made me a heroine at college, 'Dum maro dum . . . mit jaye gam . . .' I was touching guitar strings after two long years. So of course I was nervous. But when I finished playing, they gave me a round of applause. I knew it was not just my fingers. I had sung along to the playing and that must have helped.

When I finished, Ali took the guitar from me and played a few chords. I was immediately embarrassed. You know, Javed, after pretending to be a superhero among you all, it was then that I realized that what I had done so far was child's play. He was an amazing master, yaar! He especially loved to play a steel string acoustic but could also play an electric. Did those strings have such possibilities? Where did that lovely music come from – those strings or his fingers? It was no use being jealous, Javed. From when he was seven, his fingers had been trained to create magic on the strings.

He didn't come to the guitar with numb fingers like ours. I wish I could play at least one note like he does.

I was overjoyed when Ali told me I could join String Walkers. For the second time in my life, I felt validated. (The first time was when Imthiaz sir declared that I was meant to be an RJ.) Till then, my life had been circumscribed by the studio, Taya Ghar, and the flats of my uncles, but String Walkers opened a new door.

Greedy Eyes

The star of the day was actually Farhana. You wouldn't believe the boldness and sass with which she met everyone in the group. She wasn't the least shy. She went up to each person, shook hands, introduced herself, asked questions about them and joked with them and teased them. I think of myself as a confident person but she totally beat me. If nothing else, life in the big city had given her this.

And those young men, like trees uprooted in a flood, completely fell for her. Especially Ifran. They listened more to Farhana than to the song or the guitar. At one point, I wondered if they had given me membership because Farhana came with me. Only, Farah seemed to be a bit surly. Anyone could see that she was a little jealous.

'You must come again with your baji,' the men told Farhana. 'We'll teach you to play the guitar.'

As soon as Ali dropped us off, she started talking about them. 'Baji, what if I hadn't come today and missed all this? That would have been such a shame. What a terrific group. I love it.'

When we got home, I tried to set her straight. 'Look, girl, I was watching you today. Don't keep staring at men like that. They'll think you have some kind of sickness ...'

'How can I not look, baji? Did you notice Salman's stubble? Just like Aamir Khan's. And Ifran's eyes? They were like crystals. And baji, when I saw Nazar's fingers, it was all I could do not to touch them.' I realized that while we were making music, she had been drooling with desire.

She was eager to accompany me to other meetings and came along for one or two more. But each time, her behaviour seemed to get even more outrageous, and so I started making excuses to not take her. Luckily she soon started a tuition class on exactly those evenings, so it was easy to avoid her. Nawaaz also came with me a couple of times. But I put an end to that as well. I started asking for more evening shows at work. I would return home after the show and my String Walkers sessions. No one suspected anything. Our driver Yunus was a big help. But of course, no one was as skilled as Farhana at coming up with fake explanations when I wanted to leave the house in the evenings.

During one of those days, we heard that a Justin Bieber concert was to happen in the city. Farhana could not sit still after that. 'Baji, we have to go. It's my big dream to see him live. We will never have a chance like this. Baji, please, please, please,' she begged. I, too, wanted to go. But I was scared of going alone to such a crowded place. Not that there was anything to be scared of. But still. Nawaaz would come too, but he barely counted, the little coward. He was such a quiet little mouse. Completely incapable of protecting us from unwanted male attention. Besides I knew that I would have to be extra cautious going out with Farhana. She had zero discretion and would chat up random men and make a scene.

It was pointless to talk to the other men of Taya Ghar about Justin Bieber. They would probably have been like, 'Oh Bieber. You mean the Mughal king Babar? Emperor Shahjahan's father?'

So I decided to turn to Ali. I thought he would certainly be interested. I proposed the idea at String Walkers. We could all go together. It would be a fun outing for the group. And we might be able to get some free tickets through Ifran's father. So the expense was not even an issue. Everyone agreed happily. The String Walkers would go to the Bieber concert together. We would sing and dance and celebrate together.

Everyone except Ali. He declared that he would not come. Usually he would take the lead on any such plan. And now here he was, backing out of a concert! Though Hasan and Roger tried to persuade him, he wouldn't budge. 'No, no, I won't come,' he insisted. That irked everyone. I had proposed this outing excitedly because I was sure he would stand with me. Why was he, of all people, opting out?

On the way home, I kept asking Ali what the matter was, but he wouldn't explain. All he said was that one day I would understand.

The Train to Hell

One day at home, when I was bored, I went downstairs. No one was in the kitchen. A mutton curry was simmering on the stove, and when I checked, it was almost dry. I could tell that it was Aisha auntie's. I had seen bhupa leaving the house a while ago, so I knew bhupoma was all alone in her room. We call Aisha auntie bhupoma at times. I walked in without knocking. She was at the computer, which was by itself unusual. As soon as she saw me, she suddenly closed the pages she was looking at. I pretended not to notice and said, 'If you keep sitting here gazing at your computer, bhupa will have to eat dry mutton, not curried.'

'Oh no, my mutton!' She ran to the kitchen. I took the opportunity to check her browsing history. Bhupoma was looking at Facebook! You sneaky thing, I thought to myself happily. Facebook was a forbidden fruit in our household. The men of the house called it the ticket booth for the train to hell. But apparently, those tickets took only women to hell. Our men were free to delight in Facebook as much as they wanted, while we women sat patiently in heaven.

But some residents of heaven managed to find their way to hell anyway. My uncles had a beautiful Facebook friend called Nazia Hassan whose photo was that of singer Shreya Ghoshal. That's how I kept an eye on their status updates in hell. Her profile photo was that of singer Shreya Ghoshal, and her name was Nazia Hassan, and it was all made up.

I was happy to find a fellow companion on the train to hell, and one from my own family. But I did not say anything.

I let it go. Later, when I checked my account, I tried to find her profile using her name and variations of it. Nothing came up. I realized then that like me, bhupoma also had a fake name. Still, I didn't ask her about it.

I found her at her computer again another time. Pretending that I had no idea, I went and sat beside her. By then she had closed the site and was a good girl again. I looked into her eyes. She looked away guiltily. She would not meet my eye.

'Tell me the truth, bhupoma, what were you looking at?' I asked in a threatening voice.

Poor bhupoma looked frightened. She started sweating. 'Nothing at all, I was just looking at the news,' she said. Her voice was trembling as if she had committed a capital crime.

I kept my face stern. 'Weren't you looking at Facebook?'

'Me? Facebook? What is that anyway?' She tried to be defiant.

'This guilty look on your face is Facebook,' I said and hugged her. Bhupoma looked at me helplessly.

'Don't worry, I won't tell anyone. So who were you secretly checking out, my pretty little auntie?'

'No one, silly. Just trying to pass the time.'

'Oh look, your face went Facebook again. Tell me . . . aren't I your little girl?' I put my arms around her and kissed her. I knew she would fall for that.

She was silent for a minute. Then she looked around to make sure we were alone.

'I first came to Facebook to see what was so terrible about it that all the men in this house had to ban it. Just a bit of resistance against them. Then I got curious upon reading

56

other people's statuses and following the conversations that came up. Sameera, the things some women write . . . how can a woman talk so openly, despite having husbands and brothers and fathers? How can she have such deep friendships with other men? I was shocked to simply find out that such bold women existed at all. Then, I remembered a face . . . a face that had been hidden in the ashes of memory. I wondered if he was here, on Facebook. So I searched, and in the list of profiles that came up in the next five seconds, there he was. My blood curdled for a few seconds. Do you know when I had seen him last, Sameera? Sixteen long years ago. I had never thought we would find each other again. You know how young I was when I married and came here. The two of us didn't even know where the other person was. I stared at that profile photo for a long time. He had changed a lot. That bare-faced boy was now a middle-aged man. Still, I had no trouble recognizing him. He still had that mischievous smile that I loved so much. Since then, every day I have logged in and checked out his profile. I make sure he and his mischievous smile have not gone anywhere. In sixteen years of marriage, I had never recalled him even once. Your bhupa takes such good care of me. I have no need to remember him. But now I can't stop recalling and looking at his photo. Is this right or wrong? I don't know. Rather, I know it's wrong but I still do it anyway.'

'Are you good friends now?'

'Friends? Never. We have not even exchanged a single message. But his status updates, his comments, his photos – they are all his way of talking to me. Maybe he knows that I am here reading. And when I want to tell him something,

I update my status. And I hope that he's reading it. That's all I want.'

'But bhupoma, who would know if you messaged him? Why should you hide your love?' I asked.

'Love? No, that is not for me. Not in this life. But I can't bear to not see his picture. Facebook is like a magician who unearthed a chest of dreams that I had buried. And now it feels like butterflies are flying out of that chest! Life is now so much more interesting.'

I cannot even attempt to describe the way her eyes shone when she said that.

'Never mind all that. What is your fake profile name, bhupoma?'

'No way, chhoti! I will never tell you that. I need at least one secret to keep to myself.'

'Bhupoma, you forget that Facebook is a train to hell.' I faked a stern face.

'Never mind, I have decided to travel a little while on that train.' She looked like a naughty little girl.

'Bhupoma, don't tell anyone but I too have a ticket on the train to hell.'

We fell into each other's arms laughing.

Kadhim al-Jubouri

The maintenance office, where Ali worked, was in between the studio and the canteen. I would laugh whenever I saw the sign in front of his office, which said 'Authorized

Personal'. Ali didn't realize it was wrong till I pointed it out. But the sign stayed. His supervisor Abdullah Janahi was convinced that the sign was correct, never mind some silly girl who thought otherwise. I wanted to visit this office. Sometimes one just wants to visit an operation theatre, or a men's restroom or a dance bar. Just like that. So one day I disobeyed the sign, and on the way back from the canteen, dropped by Ali's office. Only Abdullah Janahi and two Indian technicians were around. They looked at me enquiringly. Perhaps I was the first woman to ever set foot in that office. 'I want to meet Ali,' I said. 'He is checking out a complaint. You can sit here and wait for him,' they said and gave me a chair. But I didn't sit. I was too busy taking in the office. It was the first time I had ever seen a technical workshop-cum-office. It was an organized place. There were a variety of tools to inspect machines on the table. Then there were some electronic boards that looked like computer motherboards. Fans, cables, microphones, a bunch of things that looked like the innards of machines. I didn't know their names. Even though I didn't understand much, I walked around touching things and looking at them. How did people figure out how to fix them? These technical workers must be really smart.

'That's where your friend Ali sits,' Abdullah Janahi said when I strayed close to a table. It was tidy. There was a sign on one side that said, 'Never promise more than you can perform.' That was Ali's motto. He would repeat it whenever we talked of the overload of work at the studio. He followed that principle in his own job. Even if the telecast was in chaos because of some studio apparatus not running properly, he did not care. There was a limit to how much a person could work. 'If I keep saying yes to make other people happy, I'll become another Sheela Garments,' he would argue.

Next to his motto, he had pasted three photos: the guitar magician Jimi Hendrix, the Kurdish singer Aynur Dogan and a fat man I did not recognize. Since I knew he was crazy about music, I was not surprised by Hendrix and Dogan, but who was the huge man who looked like a wrestler? I had no idea why this photo was relevant or interesting. Though I waited a bit longer, Ali did not turn up. So I left, telling his colleagues that it was time for me to go live. After all, the real point of the visit was to see the office, not Ali.

Another day, when we were on our way to String Walkers in Ali's car, I asked him, 'So who is the fat guy whose photo you keep on your table?'

'When did you see my table?'

'I stopped by your office one day on the way back from the canteen. You were not there, so I waited a bit and then left.'

'Sameera, that is Kadhim al-Jubouri. He is an Iraqi weightlifting champion. He is a big hero for us. Not because he got an Olympic medal or anything. Kadhim has a special place in Arab history. Do you have any idea why?'

I shook my head.

'Do you remember 9 April, the day the American military conquered Iraq? Maybe you saw a crowd of young men pouring into Firdos Square on TV? It was as if a prison door had finally opened after centuries. Kadhim al-Jubouri was

60

the brave soul who led those men. He was the first to raise the hammer and strike the statue of Saddam Hussein. That must have been sweet revenge for him. He had spent nine years in prison for daring to resist Saddam's dictatorship. Can revenge ever get better than that?'

Ali had seen the video of Iraqis destroying Saddam Hussein's statue more than a thousand times. 'It never bores me, no matter how many times I see it. It thrills me. I even felt jealous of the people of Iraq. I imagine the excitement and the energy they must have felt when they ran into the square, knowing that after years of waiting, the door to freedom was finally open. Will I ever be that lucky?' There was hope and despair in his voice.

I was silent for a minute. Then I said, 'Ali, what kind of mad talk is this? Kadhim al-Jubouri had a reason to feel that way – he lost nine years of his life. But what have you lost? Has this country ever harmed you? Don't you have a good education, a secure job and a decent income in this country? Shouldn't you be grateful to your rulers? Why would you want to bring down such peaceful, generous rulers?'

Ali gave me a harsh look and laughed. 'Things like education, job and income – if you have always led an ordinary life, then these things are important. That's all you have to aspire for. But my life is different. You have only seen one of my faces, Sameera. You only know the Ali who plays the guitar, checks into City Villa, eats burgers and pretends to be carefree. But there is another Ali inside me that you've never seen. And that Ali has a big dream. Some day I'll tell you. But not now.'

Second Class

I didn't realize until much later that my friendship with Ali had become a topic of conversation in our office. Naturally, after keeping tabs on news from around the world, I was the last to hear when I became the news. One evening, I was alone in the car on the way back home when Yunus brought it up.

'Madam, I keep hearing stuff about you and that Second Class. Be careful, madam. Gossip has a life of its own.'

I had no idea what he was saying. Second Class? Who was that? From the back seat, I leaned in towards him, like a question mark.

'That Ali Fardan, who else. It's not like the gossip is going to affect his life. He's not going to do much with it anyway. But you be careful, madam.'

I exploded. I lashed out at Yunus, letting loose the harami in me. 'Go tell those sonsofbitches that I sleep with Ali every day. If anyone has a problem with that, let them tell me to my face and I'll fix their problem for them.'

I went on and on. Yunus was too frightened to respond. But soon I felt bad – what was his fault after all? He was merely repeating what he had heard.

'Why do you call him "Second Class"? I asked Yunus when I had cooled down.' Once I heard the Malayalam Mafia also call him that.'

'Because he is a second-class citizen here, that's why. He doesn't really have citizenship in this country. Their people came from Iran long ago and have been living here illegally. His Majesty pretends not to see, so they get by. Otherwise they would all have been packed off back to Iran. We Sunnis are the first-class citizens here.'

I didn't understand half of what Yunus was saying. Some words – first class, second class, citizenship, Sunni – registered but I couldn't connect the dots.

The next day when I saw Ali in the canteen, I asked him frankly, 'Why does everyone call you Second Class?'

His smiling face suddenly turned grim. 'Who called me that?'

'Never mind who did. Tell me the reason.'

'Second class! This is how a country treats its own people. Do you know for how many years we've been suffering this discrimination? The curse of not belonging to the ruling majority! You will never understand how terrible it is till you experience discrimination in your own land. But I am not sad, Sameera. I have Shia blood in my veins and nothing is worth betraying that. Some day, we will also be acknowledged as humans . . .'

His face reddened with anger as he spoke. Then he got up and walked away in a huff.

Karbala

After that I was scared to bring up the topic again with Ali. I had no idea who Shias were and what they believed in. Till I came to this country, I had not even heard of such divisions. I was Sunni by birth but had never given it any thought. After all, I had never lived anywhere where my Sunni identity was relevant. I thought of myself as a Muslim

63

or as a Pakistani. It was only after coming to this country that I learned I had an extra identity, an occasionally useful one. Even then I did not know what the difference was and I had never bothered to find out. I had heard pardada speak of the big Sunni–Shia riot in Pakistan that happened several years before my birth and how thousands had died in it. That conflict crossed borders and eventually caused the Iran–Iraq war. That's how I first heard the word Shia. I assumed then that it was something along the lines of Hindu, Christian, Parsi. But after hearing out Ali, I wanted to know more.

But whom could I ask? When I asked Yunus one day in Cattle Class, his answer was vague, along the lines of: 'They are all kafirs, they believe in twelve imams who have nothing to do with Islam, they are idol-worshippers who pray to photos of dead imams, etc. Then I thought of our receptionist, Laila. Her nickname was 'Travelling Bakery'. She was always to be seen with a bag of baked goods, munching something or the other. Her goal in life was to marry a rich man, even if he was some old dodderer looking for a fourth wife. Sometimes she would chat up some random man in the street and conclude her conversation with, 'Look at me, I am so pretty, want to marry me?' In between recalling these marriage proposals, I had also heard her declaim the greatness of Shias. So I decided that she was the best person to talk to about this. And then one day I got my opportunity.

I was watching something on TV at home when I suddenly heard drumming on the street. When I went to the balcony, I saw a big procession of people, all dressed in black. They had black flags in their hands and amidst

them was a white horse without a rider. The loudspeakers in the vehicles blared songs of mourning. The people in the procession marched in pace with the rhythm of the songs. After each step, everyone paused and beat their chests. Hundreds of people did this at exactly the same time, perfectly synchronized. Then the drum sounded. Next step, pause, beating of the chests. It was like a military march. Some of those who were at the back of the procession were not beating their chest, but were striking their heads and backs with chains. Some even had swords with which they beat their foreheads. They were bleeding. I was frightened to see even small children in that procession. I ran inside and told baba, expecting him to join me on the balcony. But baba didn't take his eyes off the TV. 'Oh yes, the chest-beating. What's there to see?'

I went to Laila the next day to find out more. She was surprised. 'You don't know about all this? What kind of a Muslim are you?'

'To be honest, Laila, I had not even heard of such things. I learned to read the Quran, and I have read it from left to right and right to left. I know about the five pillars of Islam. Beyond that, I don't know any history.'

Laila found a trainee to take her place at the reception and we went to the canteen.

'That is pathetic. Don't go around displaying your ignorance. After Prophet Muhammad's death, peace be upon him, there was a fight among his followers about who would be the next leader. In fact, the Prophet had instructed them that one of his family members should lead the community – that was Allah's will. Since the Prophet had no sons, most of his followers agreed that his nephew and son-in-law Ali should be the rightful leader. But as Imam Ali and his family were busy making preparations for the Prophet's funeral, some dissidents disobeyed the Prophet's wishes and conspired to put someone else in power. They chose Abu Bakr, the Prophet's father-in-law, the oldest man among his followers, as the Caliph. That caused a huge schism.

'After Abu Bakr, they chose Omar and Osman as the Caliph. But Ali was chosen as the fourth Caliph. So Allah's will did come to pass, even if a little late. In fact, according to our belief, Ali is the first Caliph. We don't acknowledge Abu Bakr, Omar and Osman – they went against Allah's will.

'After Ali and the second imam, Hassan, died, the same quarrel took place again. The Shias wanted Hussain, who was Ali's son and the Prophet's grandson. But the other faction wanted someone from outside the Prophet's family. That fight was a big wound that never healed. The two factions fought in Karbala in Iraq. The followers had an army of thousands and Hussain had an army of seventy-two. You could call it a Muslim version of David versus Goliath. But in this contest, Goliath won and poor David lost. Hussain knew that he would lose. But he chose to die fighting injustice. Hussain and each one of his followers died at Karbala.

'But his resistance and death made history. He became the biggest martyr in Muslim history. For fourteen centuries, we have been remembering his sacrifice every year on Ashura, the ten days of mourning. We sing songs, beat our chests and hurt ourselves with chains and swords so that we

remember Hussain's courage and sacrifice. By wounding our bodies, we recreate Hussain's sacrifice. For a Shia, Ashura is the most sacred time of the year.

'In fact, Sameera, Ashura is not just about what we believe, it is about how we, as a minority, survive despite oppression. That's the Ashura that you mockingly call chest-beating. We are remembering our duty to fight against injustice and dictatorships. That's why the rulers here want to ban this. But for us, martyrdom equals fighting for your faith. And these rulers should remember that we have thousands of young men ready to become martyrs.'

When she said those words, her eyes glowed with the same fire that had lit up Ali's not long ago. Is Shia a faith of fire, I wondered.

The Hawk of Lebanon

One day, Ali and I were the first to arrive at the String Walkers meeting. Ifran was at a birthday party. Salman was at some music show. Farah had gone to the movies. Nazar, Roger and Sofia were on the way. As we waited, Ali took out his headphones and started listening to music. I watched him. With each line of the song, he became more and more excited. I held my ear close, it was an Arabic song. But he was lost in his music, and ignored my curiosity. When the song was over, Ali placed the headphones on my ears and hit replay. Though I didn't understand the words, it was clearly energizing. Perhaps a revolutionary song or a marching song.

I asked him about it.

'We are all crazy about this song right now,' he said. 'It's "The Hawk of Lebanon" by a Palestinian band called Firkat al-Shamal. It's about our brave leader Nasrallah. The song is super popular among the Arab youth. You haven't noticed? It's a common ringtone on our cellphones. You'll also hear it a lot on Arabic channels. It's spreading everywhere through emails and CDs. Till this song came out, Firkat al-Shamal was a small band that used to sing wedding songs. But now they are the most famous band in the region. That's how much we love Nasrallah.' There was a lot of passion in Ali's voice.

'So who is this Nasrallah?' I asked.

Ali gaped at me. He was astounded by my ignorance.

'I really don't know,' I confessed.

'You know how Ayatollah Khomeini and Gamal Abdel Nasser rewrote the political direction of the Middle East? Nasrallah is on par with them. Do you know, every day thousands of his pictures are sold in this part of the world? Women and children kiss those pictures. Young girls line up to marry him. Newborns are named after him. There are people who carry around his photo in their lockets. Or wear T-shirts with his photo on them. He is the biggest cult figure in the world after Che. He is the top leader of the Lebanese revolutionary organization, Hizbollah.'

Hizbollah? The name seemed familiar. 'Isn't that the biggest terrorist organization in the world? Are you a Hizbollah?' I asked him.

Ali smiled and started singing that song. 'Oh Nasrallah, Hawk of Lebanon, victory is with you. We stand behind you. We will never abandon you. Oh Nasrallah. Oh Nasrallah.'

I stared at him, while fear crawled up my body. Was this the same Ali who played the guitar with me and shared silly Internet jokes? I was frightened.

Another day, Ali shared a dream with me and my fears became even more real.

'These days, I keep seeing a dream, Sameera. It feels so real. And it keeps coming back. Someone is running through a tunnel of dirty water. There is a crowd chasing him. He is running with all his might. But the crowd catches him. They drag him through the dirty water, as if he were a rat. They are all in black with swords and guns. Their eyes are full of hate. They start beating the man as if he were a stray dog. "Don't beat me," the man says. "I am still the ruler of this country." That is when I see his face, a horrible strange face.

'"Oh, so you are the ruler? Then you deserve a few more of these," one among the crowd brings the man to his knees and thrashes him till he is bleeding from his mouth.

'"Don't beat me any more," the man begs. But they continue without listening to him, taking turns, hitting his shoulders, back, thighs, stomach, chest. They spit in his face. Drag him by his hair, stab his eyes, pinch his ears and nose, strangle him. Someone pulls his pants off and makes him stand on all fours. Then the attacker inserts his penis into the man's ass. The rest of the crowd cheers.

'"Do you remember? You and your police did all this to us. How can we say goodbye to you without reciprocating?"

'"Please, please, don't do this. I am in pain," the man continues to beg.

'But they have no sympathy for him. They drag him on the floor and throw mud on his face. Someone urinates on his face. Another picks up his gun. "We are going to kill you. This is your last chance to pray for your sins if you want to," the gunman says, aiming the gun at him.

"'No, no, please don't shoot," he says, crying. The gunman presses the trigger. The bullet flies, skimming the top of the ruler's head. His face goes white with terror. "Please, I will give you anything you want. Don't kill me. I will give you all the gold you want, pearls and diamonds. Money, shopping malls, half my country. No, the whole country, if that's what you want. I will run away and leave it all to you. Please don't kill me." But the gunman doesn't seem to hear. He pulls the trigger again.

'That's when I saw the face of the gunman, Sameera. It was me.'

I began to fear Ali as if he were an alien from another planet.

Kafir

You can fool some people all the time and all the people some of the time, but you cannot fool all the people all the time. Eventually, I too, was caught. Ahlaq mamu saw me getting out of Ali's car one night. Mamu didn't ask me anything then; in fact he walked me home. But by the time the sun rose the next morning, the news was all over the town. The phone calls I received that day proved that. From chachas and mamus to aunties, I have enough relatives in this town to populate a Bollywood movie. And everyone wanted to know what was going on. Each and every caller

70

asked the same questions. What happened last night? Who was the man who drove you home? What is the relationship between you two? Where did you go with him? Why did you go there? A long list of questions. What did I have to hide anyway? I told them all about String Walkers and my friendship with Ali. But instead of listening to me, the callers started scolding and advising. None of them believed that Ali and I were simply friends. In fact, most of them decided that the String Walkers was a story I had made up.

'Okay fine, so you are in love with some kafir and want to roam around the city with him. But why tell us all these lies about playing the guitar?' Sippy auntie yelled from the living room.

I could not even begin to express my rage. I was disgusted at how my life had to be put on display so that I could prove my innocence. They were questioning my integrity, trampling over my dreams. I was also mystified that even after years of living lives of freedom in this big city, none of them were able to believe in an ordinary friendship between a man and woman.

Javed, perhaps you too don't believe me when I say this, but as you are my witness, I swear that Ali and I were never in love, not even for a moment. Why would I lie about this to you? I never developed any special tenderness or respect for Ali. He was merely a typical young man from this city. His life was made up of five things – football, Facebook, guitar, burgers and Pepsi. I have said this to his face, half-jokingly and half-seriously, and with a laugh he admitted that I was right. I liked Ali. He was a good guitarist and a great friend. But he was not the man I wanted in my life.

71

And it was the same for him. He never told me anything otherwise. All the rest was simply the fantastic suspicion of my family. But it is true that our friendship ran deep. I told him about my menstrual cramps. He told me about having sex with a white woman. We emailed each other sleazy Internet jokes. Looking back, it seems to me that our relationship was dignified and mature, and also somehow reckless. It is difficult to understand it from the perspective of an older generation's friendships. It cannot be interpreted with the tools of an older era. But Javed, I would like to believe that you can understand our friendship. In this new era, friendship has wide open doors.

I knew that the problem was not that I had travelled alone with a young man or that he was an Arab. Some women in our own family had married Arabs. We looked upon them as fortunate women who had won the lottery. Had I, like Laila auntie who married an Englishman in Dubai, or Fathima who eloped with a Parsi in Faridabad, been in love with a European or a Parsi or a Hindu or a Jew, my family would not have objected this strongly. What really scared my aunts and uncles was that Ali was a Shia. That's when I realized that Shias were not just second-class citizens in the City, they were kafirs to be detested like hell.

Religion

This harami is confused – why is God silent, like a guilty criminal, when the contradictions of religion are exposed?

Who are your real followers, in a world where each

person claims to be right? Who did you give your sceptre to? Who strayed? Whose minds faltered? Who got greedy for power? Who went against your will? Who concealed your wishes from the people? Who is right – the minority or the majority? Does something become true simply because the majority believes in it? If so, why doesn't this country accept that? Why do we fight in your name and call each other kafirs? If there is only one truth, why didn't we all follow that one truth? What right do governments have to divide and designate people as official followers and dissidents? Just because a government is in power and has managed to rule over its people for a long time, does that give it the right to brand some people rebels?

Oh omnipotent one, if these questions are absurd, please forgive me from the depths of your mercy. If only you had given us a set of final instructions, just as you had sent other messages to the world, your children would not be swimming in rivers of blood, from Karbala to Kandahar. They would be ruling the earth instead. Did your hand falter in this, just as in the creation of man? Or is it your cruel intention that man must always fight with his brothers?

My small intelligence cannot grasp all of this. But I do know that the water is murky. No one can see clearly through it. Anyone can catch whatever fish they want in this murky water. And there are some who have a vested interest in keeping the water like this, so they can keep catching the fish of their fantasies. I cannot change their point of view. My taya, baba, mamus and chachas all have their own beliefs and they are convinced they are right. They will never understand Ali. While Ali, Hasan and Muneer

Gazi have their own beliefs and would not understand my family either. When will the day come when people start looking at things from the other person's point of view? Maybe then the water will be less murky.

Taya asked me to come to his room that night. That was not typical. I realized that I was on trial. I did not even have to make a deposition; they had already questioned Nawaaz and Farhana. So taya already knew that String Walkers was not a lie. But he was still apprehensive about my relationship with Ali. Though I swore up and down that it was not what they suspected, he did not believe me. It was as if he wanted me to confess that I was in love with Ali. I stopped resisting. What was the point anyway?

'It is natural at your age to develop these kinds of feelings.' Taya's voice changed as he said this. 'But I made enquiries about him and the information is not good. Isn't he your good friend? Have you tried to find out who he really is?'

'I know he is a kafir,' I said, giving taya the answer I thought he was expecting.

'If that was all, I would have borne it for you.' Taya's response surprised me. 'If you still don't understand, let me spell it out. He is a Hizbollah. A killer dog that might fall to our bullets any time. You want to love someone like that?'

Ali? Hizbollah? A suicide bomber whose mission in life was to kill and be killed? My head went woolly. I remembered the song he sang about Nasrallah. When I had questioned him, he had dismissed me with a laugh. But now . . . I knew that there were suicide bombers in the world. But I had always thought of them as poverty-stricken Afghanis or illiterates from my own country or religious fanatics from Yemen. Money and ignorance and religion had turned them towards the drug of death. But Ali? An educated young man from a wealthy country. How did he become a Hizbollah? I had to know.

Papa Kehte Hain

There was one person who did not participate in the ruckus that took place in those days and that was baba. Amidst all the advice I got from my chachas and mamus, and even after taya's inquisition, baba did not ask me anything. That did not mean that he was unaware of what was happening or that he was not worried about it. But baba hesitated to ask me anything. Perhaps he was afraid he could not bear it if I responded in anger.

The day after my meeting with taya, baba told me, 'Come, let's go out.' I had no idea why. We went to the souk. 'I don't believe anything they say. I trust you,' baba said on the way. The relief I felt then. Even if the entire world blamed me, it didn't matter. Baba's faith in me was all I needed. I turned into a small child again. After years, I put my hand in his.

We stopped in front of Echoes, a famous music shop in the souk. It was a big showroom that sold musical instruments.

'I used to always wonder at how your eyes widened whenever we passed this shop,' baba said as we walked in. 'I never knew that you had such a love for music.'

'Did ma never tell you?'

'No, she never tells me anything. Especially about our children.'

I had assumed that ma must have told him about finding a guitar in my room.

'Okay, now choose a guitar for yourself as a gift from me.' When baba uttered those words, I was ecstatic. To hear that from baba was like entering heaven itself.

The shop had an extensive collection of guitars. I had long lusted after Yamaha's Electric Series. But knowing the limitations of baba's pocket, I picked an ordinary acoustic.

From when we paid for it at the counter till we got back home, baba carried my guitar. Even when I offered to carry it, eager to touch it, he refused. And to all the acquaintances he saw on the way, he proudly said, 'This is for my daughter, she knows how to play this.' Only after we got home did I get to hold it.

After dinner I went off to wash the dishes. When I returned, baba was fiddling with the strings, as if he were a little kid. He looked chagrined when I spotted him. 'Play something,' he requested. Javed, there isn't a single moment in my life when I felt prouder. That moment, I was validated by my own father.

You remember that old song we sang a lot during our college days? Aamir Khan's 'Papa kehte hain bada naam karega, beta hamara aisa kaam karega'. That's the song I sang for baba that night. Except, instead of 'beta', I sang 'beti'. When I finished, baba went to the balcony without a word. When I followed him there, wondering if he hadn't liked my singing, I found him crying.

I didn't know how to comfort him. I was seeing another face of the father I had always feared.

Nathoor

It was taya, of course, who had brought baba to the City and found him a job. In those days, there was a post called Nathoor in the police department of this country. It was the lowest rung in the police force. Basically a security guard. The main responsibility is to stand guard in front of government offices, schools and embassies. Till I came here, all I knew was that baba had a job in the police department. In fact, we used to grumble back home that our baba lived such a simple life in the same city where his brother was a well-off, influential policeman. Taya must not care much for us, we thought.

It was after I came here that I understood what baba's job was really about. In the early days, baba did not make enough to provide for his family in such an expensive city. By the time he was able to, ma was no longer interested in joining him. As the head of her house, ma had built an independent universe for herself. A universe in which she did not have to bow to her husband's authority, a universe in which she could spend money as she wished, a universe in which she could order about her children and servants. When baba came on his usual thirty days of leave, greedy for time with his family, ma always seemed uncomfortable. Her days of freedom were being curtailed briefly. Eventually she simply stopped imagining a future in which she joined him in the City or he returned to us in the village. When we speak of the loneliness of those who live alone, we must also remember the freedom of living alone. After the initial difficulty, the person living alone begins to prefer loneliness.

Of course, when baba was away, ma kept lamenting his absence. She complained to everyone – to guests, relatives, dogs and cats on the street – that baba was alone in a foreign country with no one to take care of him, no one to attend to his meals or his laundry. She would weep and pray and mourn her fate. But the day he arrived for his vacation, she would become uneasy. By the third day, she would start finding fault with him. And she would get us involved as well. There is a special relationship between children and a mother raising them single-handedly. We isolated that man who arrived once in a while as a guest and tried to slip into his father role. We teased him. We baited him with our words. We laughed at his clothes and his poor English. We even laughed at him for visiting the bathroom more than once a day.

We were a tribe defending ourselves. We did not want anyone to rein in the special freedoms we enjoyed. We continued in this manner till baba left. I don't think baba ever felt content when he went back to the City. It was more as if he had somehow escaped us. I remember one incident in particular.

One day at home when we, including ma, were teasing him, baba burst into tears. He felt small about his ignorance and helplessness. I was twelve or thirteen then. For my birthday, baba had sent me a card that played music when you opened it. It was the first time in my life that baba had sent me a greeting card. He had no interest in 'fashionable' behaviours like expressing love, sending greeting cards or paying compliments. But perhaps some friends of his had fired him up: 'Your daughter is growing up fast, if you don't show her love now, when will you?' And so he had eagerly gone to some shop and bought a card and sent it to me on my birthday. That's not why we laughed at him. The card baba had sent me for my birthday was a Christmas card!

Recollecting this incident, Sameer, ma and I poked fun at baba. For a while baba did not give in. But then he suddenly burst into tears. I did not have the maturity to understand then that we were laughing at baba's innocence. And ma did not have the wisdom or even common sense to teach us that. Later, I cried many times wondering how much we must have wounded him. From that day, I started loving baba anew. Till then, I had thought of baba as a bogeyman. At least three times a day ma would threaten us: 'You wait till baba comes home, this arrogance of yours will end then.' She had always portrayed him as a visiting monster.

Only after I emerged from ma's circle of influence did I truly understand how much we had isolated baba. To be exact, it was only after I started living with him. But by then, baba had learned to keep his distance from us. There was always love and affection. But he did not attempt to establish any clout over me as a father. Perhaps he had forgotten that this was his due. Maybe that was why he had never brought up the question of my marriage. Maybe that was why he always went to my uncles when he wanted help with disciplining me.

Today I opened baba's box. This is my first time seeing what was inside. There were two brand new pyjamas. Ma had bought them for him the last time he visited. He had not even touched them, content with his old clothes and pyjamas. Below that was a package bound thoroughly in plastic. I opened it. It was a salwar in ma's favourite pink colour. He must have bought it to give to her on his next visit. Also in the package was a small packet of almonds, a face cream, two black bras, a tin of Yardley lavender powder. And then, a half-bitten sweet samosa! All of ma's favourite things. I sat down in shock. Who was my baba? Like the demon in the story, he had locked up all his love in his heart and had been safeguarding it. For whom did he live so frugally, so carefully? Had he, in fact, ever lived at all?

Khan

Khan is a clan name that goes all the way back to the Turkic and Mongol races. But all the Khans we see today did not get their name from there. Many received the name as an honorific. The Khan in my baba's and dada's names were such titles. My dada had been a high-ranking officer in the British infantry. The British had honoured him with the Khan title for his service.

Even now, on a wall of our house, there is a black-and-white photo of dada standing proudly in a splendid army uniform, wearing all his medals. He had the kind of handsome figure no one could resist looking at. Dadi would boast every now and then that he had three wives and four mistresses. Not only that, she exhorted her own sons from time to time: 'How can you be satisfied bumbling along with just one wife? Go be a man like your baba and get two or three wives.' Of dada's five sons, it was only taya who inherited a small portion of that handsomeness and even he was nothing compared to dada. The legacy of dada's beauty completely skipped my own baba and the other sons.

But while dada flourished as a Khan in the British army, my own baba's fate was to be a foot soldier in some other country.

When I was a child, we all believed that everyone who lived in the Arab lands owned at least one oil well. We assumed that all they had to do was draw some oil and sell it to live their lavish lives. Arabs did not need to do any of their own chores. And that was why my taya and baba and uncles worked as policemen in their countries. It was only after I arrived here that I realized that this country was ruled by His Majesty and my taya and others were protecting his administration. Their job was not to defend the country from foreign invaders, it was to protect His Majesty from his own people, in the name of law and order. What a paradox.

For a long time, baba was a security guard at the Syrian embassy. Then he moved to the gate of the Moroccan embassy. A few years ago, the government cancelled the Nathoor posts and promoted everyone to the armed forces. If that hadn't happened, baba would have still been an ordinary Nathoor. And I wouldn't have lost him.

Hizbollah

I had a recurring nightmare around then. Ali and I are leaving some office. We walk together to the lift lobby. But when the lift arrives, we step into two different lifts. It doesn't matter, we'll reach there at the same time, I tell myself. But my lift stops en route on a couple of floors and reaches the ground floor late. The ground floor of the office building is a railway station. Ali reaches before I do and gets into a train thinking I am with him. I arrive after him and run into a train, thinking he is on it. But after a few minutes of travel, we call each other on the phone and realize that we are on different trains. Don't worry, get off at the next station, Ali says, we can meet there. Then we realize that our trains are moving in two different directions, that we can never get off again at the same station. I wake up from my nightmare when I jump out of that train that will never stop.

I have had this nightmare many times. I had no idea what my subconscious was afraid of, what it was trying to say. But I knew that each dream was a clue. One day I ran into Ali in the market. After the problems with my family, I had not seen Ali or gone to any String Walkers meetings. He, too, had been busy. At the studio, I avoided him as much as possible. Perhaps he understood. But now he invited me to walk with him. I couldn't say no. We went to a cafe and then sat in a park talking.

We had to cross a highway to get back to the car park. It was not a busy time, and we could have easily crossed the highway. But he wouldn't do it. We walked a bit further and then crossed over on a footbridge. I couldn't understand why he was so afraid of crossing a road. As we walked to the car, he explained.

'When I was a child, my brothers and friends used to play a little game. Running across the highway when vehicles were coming at top speed. Even now my feet tingle when I think of that game. But back then, it was exciting. I was always the winner at running across three-lane highways. Some vehicles would almost touch us as they passed. And some other vehicles had to brake so quickly they burnt their tyres. I still remember the high I got when I left my friends behind on one shore and ran across to reach the other. It was full of arrogance, that high. We would play that game for hours. But one day it ended in a tragedy. My brother lost the game. He did not reach the other shore. A Benz car that was racing down the street hurtled into him. Even now I have a bruised memory of his scream and the way the glass windows of the car were splattered with blood. You know, Sameera, one of the reasons I became friends with you is because of your name. My brother was called Sameer. You remind me of him. It's not what your chachas think – that I am in love with you. That's not the kind of life I want. I am setting my life aside for something else . . .'

If he had said then that he was in love with me, I would have accepted his love. The opposition at home from my uncles and aunts was actually bringing me closer to him, rather than pushing me further away.

I looked into his eyes and asked, 'Will you tell me the truth about something?'

'There are two kinds of cowardice in the world: the cowardice of too much power and the cowardice of too much money. Since I have neither power nor money, I am not afraid of anyone and I don't have to lie,' Ali answered.

'Let me ask you this, then. Are you a Hizbollah?'

He gazed at me for a minute. Then he laughed.

'Listen Sameera, I am not political and I don't follow any ideology and there is no religion in my head. History teaches us the dangers of these things. But I still respect them because they try to solve human problems. I am not from Hizbollah or Quds or Hamas or Al-Qaeda or the Taliban. I have not given my life to any of those. But I do know what my life has taught me. And because of that, I want those who are in power now to fall down and shatter. I have my reasons for that . . .'

Though I didn't understand all that he said, that conversation helped melt the icy silence that had crept between us. We became friends again. I stopped caring what other people thought.

The Donkey Cart and the Mercedes

Around that time, an incident shook a neighbouring city. It began with the police arresting two young brothers who were riding a donkey cart through one of the main avenues of the city, selling fruits and vegetables. One of them was an engineering student and the other was a medical student, both working part-time as vegetable vendors to fund their education. A policewoman stopped them and reprimanded them for bringing shame to the country and its ruler by riding a donkey cart through such an important road, one used by foreigners and tourists. The young men said that they did not have a Mercedes car to ride through the streets and safeguard the nation's honour. If the donkey cart caused the rulers such shame, they should feel free to buy a Mercedes car for the vegetable vendors, the police were told. In a country where the words His Majesty could only be said with respect, the policewoman found their talk to be nothing short of sedition. She arrested them and took them to the police station where the young men were beaten up. The police released them that evening but kept their donkey and the cart. The next day, when the young men went to the station, the donkey cart was gone. When they asked the senior police officers about it, they got a sarcastic response: 'We drowned it in the sea.'

Selling vegetables had been the only source of livelihood for the two young men. They went to the mayor of the city. He replied that the donkey cart had to be seized because they were breaking the Business Act of the country by running a vegetable business without a licence. The young men returned home. The next day, the younger brother immolated himself in front of the mayor's mansion just as the mayor was exiting his car.

This was the kind of incident that no one would have heard of in a country such as this. But someone who saw this incident took a video on his phone and uploaded it on YouTube. From there, it arrived on Facebook where it was viewed and shared widely. Within minutes, the anger spread. Thousands of young people demonstrated in front of the medical college where Jasim, the younger brother, was on his deathbed. The crowd prayed for his life and raised slogans against the rulers.

The rulers had to do something. His Majesty visited Jasim and promised him whatever help he needed. The incident would be investigated, His Majesty declared. But fate had other plans. In four days, Jasim died in the hospital.

That incident was the germ of a revolution that spread like a fever from city to city.

Part 3

Muryoon

Virtual Revolutions

As is the body, so is the body politic: if you touch a reflex spot, the body politic will react.

The news that the protests were coming to our City spread like a sandstorm. At the canteen, all conversations were about the revolution. Ali and his friends started a Facebook group to share their thoughts and continue the conversations through constant status updates and discussions. The majority of the locals who posted there wanted to start protesting. But they argued about when, where and how. I found this funny, and puzzling. In any other city, it would have been justified if a young man spoke about revolution. The situation was bad in many places. But here, in this City, what did they lack? What would they protest? Were they starving? Were they unemployed? A bunch of dudes whose life circled around Facebook and eating burgers – what would they protest? What did these idiots even hope to achieve? And anyway, what was the point of a protest without politicians and parties?

One day in the canteen I teased Ali about his protests.

'So you have abandoned City Villa and Social War for the revolution? Or is the revolution the latest Facebook game?'

'Just you wait – you'll soon find out what is a game and what is real.'

I laughed. 'Yeah, yeah. You think you can create a virtual revolution, like how you build on City Villa without lifting a finger or win at Army Attack without spilling any blood. But don't forget – the result of a virtual revolution will also be virtual.'

Ali remained confident. 'Something's going to happen in the City. One day I am going to run through the streets of this city just like Kadhim al-Jubouri ran through the streets of Iraq to destroy Saddam's statue.'

'But Ali, I still don't understand. What can you possibly gain from this revolution? You and Muneer have good government jobs, the kind of salary that is unimaginable even in a democracy, great benefits . . . Do you want to risk losing all this?'

He smiled at me. There was a tinge of mockery in that smile. 'Sameera, this is what small-minded people all over the world are asking – why should the man who has money want a revolution? But is a revolution for the sake of money? I don't know how to explain all the circumstances to you. Let me just say one thing though. Money is not the issue here. You said that I have a government job. But do you know, many of us are not counted as citizens and do not have even basic fundamental rights because we are Shias? We are not allowed to leave the country. There are professions that are completely closed to us. There are defined limits to what a Shia can achieve in this country. However smart he is, he will

90

not be allowed to go beyond those limits. Maschinas, who is a Cypriot, can become the director of a radio station such as ours. No problem. But a Shia who lives in this country could not even dream of that.

'Why do you think your baba and uncles are here? Do you know any other country where the army is full of coolie soldiers from other countries? Which country is His Majesty defending himself from? His own country. The rented soldiers are here to defeat his own people. It doesn't matter how well we behave, how much we express our patriotism, how much we declare our love for His Majesty – we could never join the army or the police. Because we are Shias. This is life as a second-class citizen. I am sure there are many countries where minorities experience discrimination at the hands of their governments. But is there any other country in the world where the majority is oppressed by a minority? Where a minority denies the majority basic rights? Shouldn't we fight against this injustice?'

'Don't be annoyed at my questions. I am just asking about the things I have heard. But aren't you Shias also immigrants like us? What right do you have to question the rulers?'

'No, I am not annoyed. And indeed, there is an allegation that we came here from Iran. But in reality, we are not immigrants. It's completely false, this belief that Shias originated in Iran and that all Shias must have come from there. In fact, the original rulers of Muslim Arabia, the Qarmatiya clan and the Uyunid clan, were Shia. The City used to be an important centre of Shia life. And the Usfurids and the Jarvanids, who were in power till the sixteenth century when the Portuguese came, were also Shias. So for eight centuries, from the beginning of Islam, it was the Shias who ruled this part of the world. To say that there were no Shias here and all the Shias must have come running here from Iran . . . only children who don't know history would believe that.

'The Portuguese ruled this city only for eight years. The Safavids of Iran scattered them and ruled the City for 115 years. It was only in 1717, when the Omani clan started taking over, that the Sunnis started dominating this country.

'Do you see now that we are the original people of this land and that this city belongs to us? And now we are asking for it to be returned to us. It's stupid to think of this as the arrogance of insurgents. Think about the paradox. We, who have lived here from time immemorial, have become second-class citizens while those who came after us have become the rulers. Why should we accept this?'

I asked Ali one more question. 'Isn't the real issue money? Isn't the revolution actually fuelled by jealousy towards the wealthy?'

'No, Sameera, it is not about money. You seem to think that a revolution is about squabbling for money. Poverty can destroy hope, depress, disappoint and breed envy. That is what is happening in some of our neighbouring countries. And that can turn into an internal conflict between the haves and the have-nots. But that is different from the confidence and sense of justice that emerges from a deep understanding of your selfhood. The knowledge that I have every right to be your equal – that is not the same as the have-nots feeling jealous of the haves. And that self-knowledge will lead to the real revolution. That is where we are now. And when you understand that, you will understand why we are protesting.'

I stared at him. 'Do you have any hope that this revolution will succeed?'

'No, I have no guarantee that we will win. But we can't live in fear of defeat. What matters is not what we will eventually achieve, what matters is what we did. History should not think of us as those who missed the opportunity to act.'

Ali brimmed with confidence. Nothing I said could have changed his mind.

The Third One

A young man at a nearby table who had been listening to our conversation approached us. I had seen him watching us. We fell silent as he came up.

'May I sit with you for a bit?' he asked.

We did not object. He started talking to us. 'I have been listening to your conversation. Not deliberately at first. But when I overheard you, I couldn't help listening. This is one of my favourite topics. I am not here to advise you and I certainly don't know who is right. That's not what I am interested in. But I want you to hear my life story.

'I am an Iraqi. I have been a refugee in this land for several years. I came here because I didn't have any other option after suffering through the Iraq war and the internal violence that erupted after the war. I have two grouses against the Americans. First, they invaded my country and destroyed it. But what was worse, they made a hero out of Saddam. He died a dignified death. That's not how he should have died. We wanted him to die on the streets. We wanted to beat him like a dog, tie him to a donkey cart, and put an iron rod up his ass before we killed him. We wanted to give him the same punishment the people had given Colonel Gaddafi. That's how much he had tortured us. That's how much we hated him. But you know what, Iraq without him is worse off than Iraq with him.

'Of course it is important to rebel against dictators. Those rebellions must succeed. But if the people of a country divide themselves along sectarian lines, then the situation after the fall of the dictator will be a nightmare. Do you know how horrible it is to view your own neighbours with terror and suspicion? I am a Sunni who lived in a Shia-majority region. When the violence broke out and Sunnis started getting attacked, I took a Shia name and got a fake ID card. With heavy hearts, we raised black Shia flags above our house and put up pictures of Shia imams in our living rooms. Somehow, we managed to keep the Shias and their Mahdi army at bay. But our tragedy did not end there. The Sunni fundamentalists came to our streets. Their targets were not Shias, instead they were hunting down Sunnis who were leading fake lives. They considered us traitors to the religion, those who had strayed from the right path. They did not try to understand the circumstances under which we had to choose these fake lives.

'We lived in a terrifying confusion. Was the man asking us for an ID on the street a policeman or a terrorist in police uniform? And if he was a terrorist, was he Sunni or

Shia? If he was Shia and we showed our Sunni IDs, death was certain. And if he was Sunni and we showed our Shia IDs, then too it would be death. Sometimes I tossed a coin before showing my ID. You will not understand the pain and terror I experienced at such moments. Only those who have walked the same streets will understand.

'And don't think you can report such terrorists to the police. One day these terrorists wore police uniforms and visited every house in the village, distributing pamphlets that said if we saw or suspected terrorist activity, we should report it to the police. Then they tapped our phones to find out who was calling the police. Those who called the police were killed in the streets. My brother who went to the market one day never returned. I still don't know whose gun killed him. How could we continue in such a land? We abandoned everything we had and took refuge here, hoping there would be peace for us here. And so my friends, that is my experience. If a country is going to be split along communal lines, it is far better to be under a dictator. You have only lost your freedom so far. But if the dictator falls, you will lose your peace and your life itself.

'Never mind Iraq. That was our fate. Think of Tunisia and Egypt and Libya. Did you see how the Islamic extremists who were on the fringes till then completely hijacked the revolution when the people of those countries took to the streets against the dictators who had kept them in poverty and injustice? Have you noticed the developments in those places now that the dictators are gone? Do you know that they are trying to implement the Sharia in the name of democracy? Maybe you would argue now – what's wrong with that if that's what the people want, those are democratically elected governments. Don't forget that Hitler, Saddam, Hosni Mubarak and Gaddafi also came to power through elections. We know what happened to those democracies. I can hear you think: "But this is different. What's so bad about the Sharia?" Nothing at all. That's Allah's law and I respect it. But the fanatics who are in charge of executing the law do not know what they are doing. If they come to power, don't think that you can sit together like this and have a chat. You cannot even sing a song. They will control your lives.

'I don't know if you would believe what I am about to say, but I will say it anyway. Recently, in my country, in Iraq, two young men selling vegetables were killed in front of their shop. It was not because they had committed an act of sedition. The accusation against them was that they had violated Islamic laws.

'We might be able to comprehend why barbers are killed for cutting hair in un-Islamic ways. Why mobile phone shopkeepers are killed for selling phones with Western music for ringtones. Why the electronics shop owner is killed for selling a dish antenna. But vegetable vendors? Their crime was that they had displayed cucumbers and tomatoes side by side in their store. Tomatoes are like vaginas and cucumbers represent penises, so it is now a crime to set them next to each other. When I spoke to a friend recently, he told me the situation was even more pathetic. Bananas have to be sold in plastic covers now. Male goats have to wear underwear. And there's a fatwa against ice. Because 1400 years ago, during the Prophet's time, there was no ice, so we too, should not use ice. What do you think of this progress? Is this the kind of society you want to create through your revolution?

'Either the permissive societies of the West or the extremism of Muslim fundamentalists – there are only two poles on the earth right now. There should be a middle way between these two. But till that middle path becomes possible, it's better to let the dictators rule. Otherwise your life will become even more terrible. A person who can think for himself cannot as easily bid goodbye to the twenty-first century and go and live in the seventh century.

'Friend, I heard you bring up our old hero Kadhim al-Jubouri at some point. Do you know what he says now? "I regret destroying Saddam's statue. These sectarians are worse than the dictator. Each new day is more horrible than the previous one." This is not just Kadhim's lament, it is each and every Iraqi's thought.'

That night I messaged Ali on Facebook. 'It is easy to destroy a statue. Building a new one is hard work. Happy Valentine's Day.'

Weekend Revolutions

We heard about the revolution spreading from city to city, like a deadly virus. But in our own city, we only felt it in the form of a few small traffic blocks. Now and then, some opposition groups conducted protests with the permission of the rulers. They often chose weekends for such protests and we laughed at such demonstrations. More than anything else, they seemed to function as recreational activities after six days of work.

But as the days passed, the traffic blocks became longer. Our cars began to crawl slower than before. Soon traffic blocks became something that could appear on any street at any time. Each day, the protest was in a different street. So a road that was free and open the previous day could be endlessly congested the next day. No one knew what road to take in the evening to get home. You had to call those who had left earlier to find out where the roads were open. Even then, Yunus would be driving towards a supposedly free road when suddenly the blue lights of the traffic police cars would appear in front of him, blocking that road and redirecting traffic.

'Madam, the roads don't go home any more, they go where the police want us to go. No point telling them our destination is not in the direction they are pointing towards. Best to just leave here. Let's see where we reach,' Yunus would complain.

We had a programme that provided live traffic updates. Listeners called in with info about traffic blocks. But strangely enough, Javed, in those days, when the roads of the City were knotted with traffic, we could not tell our audience about it. Not because we did not get updates but because there were too many blocked roads. Also, there were strict orders from the higher-ups: no traffic updates.

A few days later, there were reports of clashes between the police and the protesters in some villages. We heard about tear gas and lathi charges. That was a hint that the revolution had spread from the cities to the villages. Yunus mocked the news: 'Oh, these villages of theirs. The protests will die right there. They won't go beyond their villages.'

But I had never seen Ali happier. I asked him once, why is your face glowing? He replied, 'You and your generation did not have the good fortune to see your country waking into freedom. That was the lot of your father and his father. But in this country, my generation will get that opportunity.'

The revolution became stronger. 'On 14 February, we will all gather in the city square. We will leave only after that ruling vulture steps down,' Ali said to me. He was inspired by similar protests in other cities.

The protests were a good example of the butterfly effect in chaos theory. A butterfly beating its wings in the Amazon forest can set off a storm in New York City. Perhaps Jasim had never imagined that his suicide could have dragged entire cities into an angry, cross-border revolution. The smallest action can have unpredictable consequences.

Ahmedo

One day, I needed to leave the studio a little earlier than usual. But there were no vehicles. I was contemplating calling a taxi when I saw Ali about to leave in his car and he offered me a ride into town.

As usual, the Kurdish musician Aynur Dogan was singing 'Ahmedo' in his car. This song is a constant in Ali's CD player. This might be the song that Ali has listened to the most in his life. He does not know Kurdish and he has no idea what the song is about. But still he listens to this song greedily. There is something haunting and wounding in it that makes you listen to it on repeat.

'Why do you like this song so much?' I asked him. I had been meaning to ask him about it for a while.

He was silent for some time. Then he asked, 'Are you in a hurry to get home?'

'No, as long as I get home by four, it's okay.'

'Okay, let's give a ride to someone,' he said and turned into a different road. He drove us to the CID office in the city. There, a woman was waiting for him. A middle-aged woman with melancholic eyes. She got into the back of the car.

'This is my mother,' Ali introduced her.

I turned around in surprise. So this was Ali's mama. He had spoken of her a lot during our trips to String Walkers sessions.

'Mama, this is the Sameera that I was telling you about. She plays the guitar,' Ali introduced me and I smiled at her deferentially. Except for a pale smile, there was no response from her. She stared outside with empty eyes. I wondered if she was annoyed with me for sitting like a queen in the front seat of her son's car.

As soon as he dropped her off, I scolded Ali.

'Why didn't you tell me you were giving a ride to your mother? I would have got off first.'

'Why? She has been wanting to meet you for a while. This must have made her happy.'

'Yeah, right, why didn't she say a word to me then? She must be so annoyed.'

'No, it is not you, today she can't speak to anyone,' Ali

said. 'Today is a day of emptiness for her. One of many such days.'

I stared at him uncomprehending.

'You asked me why I like that Ahmedo song so much. It is because there is an Ahmedo inside me.'

I stared at him silently. Then he told me a story.

'In 1992, when the big war was happening, one night my poor baba went out to buy some kuboos. On the way, a police vehicle stopped him for no reason and the policeman asked him where he was going. He said that he was going to buy some kuboos. The next question was: "Are you Sunni or Shia". Baba answered angrily that he had been living in this village for twenty-seven years and no one had ever asked him that question. The policeman's response was to hit him on the head with his bayonet. Baba questioned that too. The policemen got out of the car and beat him up mercilessly, while everyone on the street stared. Then he dragged him into the police car and took him away. Sameera, my father never returned. Since then, baba is just a dream for me and my mother and my two older sisters. A dream that he will come back some day. Some people say that they drowned him alive in the sea. Others say that they beat him to death in the jail. Yet others say that he is still alive in a secret prison in a neighbouring country. After all these years, we haven't received any news of baba.

'When they took baba away, I was three years old. After dropping off my sisters at school, mama would take me to the CID office and stand in front of it, holding me. She was hoping for some news from some officer who might glance out through a window. That became her daily routine.

I grew up in front of that CID office. There were many other women there, like my mama. And many children like me. In fact, some days it was so crowded with women and children that mama wouldn't even reach the door. Then she would cry all the way home. When I asked her why, she had no answer, and I was too young to understand. One of my earliest memories is of a police officer walking out of that door and mama stopping him. She put me in front of the officer and said, 'You can go after you tell me where his baba is.' I have never seen so much courage in my mama, before or ever since. But that officer shoved me out of his way and kept walking. That fall, that is my oldest memory. After all these years, I still remember lying on the street and seeing the arrogance in his eyes. Whenever I see a policeman, I remember the face of the one who shoved me that day.

'For years, mama continued to take me to that office, hoping against hope that baba's name would appear on some list of those who had been captured or released or punished. Every day she would scour the noticeboards where such lists were published. But we never saw his name. Even after nineteen years of waiting, mama is still hopeful. Today as well she had gone to the office hoping to find some news of baba. For a few days now, she won't be able to talk to anyone. That's my mama. Hope incarnate. Also disappointment incarnate.

'"Ahmedo" is a song about a boy who is parted from his father. The singer is asking the boy, "Will you ever meet your father?" That's why I like this song so much.

'Those days, when mama used to crowd around the noticeboard with other women, I sat and played in the mud underneath. I found a playmate there, our Hasan. His baba too had gone missing. He never came back from work one day. After a lot of searching, they found his car in a corner of an isolated gali. No one knows how his father disappeared. There are so many of us like that. There's a group of us now, who found each other in front of the CID office. We call ourselves the "Sons of Missing Fathers".

'Sameera, every other hatred can slowly fade away. But when innocents are tortured, that hatred only grows more with time. The agonies our fathers and uncles went through simply because they were born as Shias. The loneliness of our mothers. How can we forget all that? Our lives were built on their stories of tears. Those stories groomed us to hate, to avenge.

'I dream of destroying something somewhere. It goes back to that day when that police officer pushed me aside. For twenty years, that dream has been brewing like a volcano inside me. I have been eyeing some statues that I want to destroy. Statues of our rulers in brave poses. Whenever I pass such a statue, I murmur to it, you are standing up now so that I can break you one day. Sometimes, when I drive through the outer highways, I can see the mountains of our rulers' mansions peeping out from behind tall walls. I dream that one day, like the Russian revolutionaries who leaped into the palaces of the tsars, like the Islamic revolutionaries who ran into the Shah of Iran's palace, I too will scale those walls and run into those mansions.

'My grandfather used to tell us a legend about our people. We were born into a race of ants called Muryoon. They live silently underneath the big buildings of the city. No one sees them. But every single ant is working hard. Each one removes grains of sand from the skeleton of the building. Through a tiny hole, as big as the eye of a needle, they take the grain out. One day, you will hear of a big building collapsing for no reason. We are those ants, Sameera, removing the grains of sand from under the authorities. One day you will hear the collapse. I hope it happens in my lifetime. But even if it doesn't, I will not be disappointed. I will sing this dream into my son's ears. I will tell him stories of his grandfather who disappeared one night when he went to buy bread. I will not let this dream blow out.'

That night, Ali wrote on Twitter: 'Your Majesties, Excellencies and Highnesses: we spit on you.'

His Majesty

From the balcony of our flat, we can see a billboard on a skyscraper bearing a gigantic picture of His Majesty, his hands waving to an invisible crowd. I am afraid of that picture. He has a vulture's sharp eyes and a cruel, beaked nose. One cannot look at that picture for too long.

Mr Vulture came to power forty years ago and hasn't allowed any democratic processes in all this time. He often declares that Allah appointed him the ruler of his people, and so it was not necessary to ask for the people's will. Though he listens to all his advisers, he never accepts any of their advice. He makes his own path. A story about him goes like this: he was travelling by car with an adviser from the left wing and another from the right wing. At a junction, the driver asked which way he should go. The left wing adviser said left and the right wing adviser said right. Mr Vulture asked the driver to turn on the left indicator and go right.

Some see Mr Vulture as the saviour of the country. It is under his tenure that the country attained all this progress. It has to be admitted that he did take this country, which was all desert and swamp, to the heights of development. Excellent roads, a first-class airport, tall buildings, beautiful gardens, electricity and drinking water and sanitation facilities . . . he changed the face of the country.

So then, why did so many people want a change of rule? I asked Yunus about this one day when we were alone in the car. I wanted to know what he thought. He laughed like an idiot when he heard my question. I couldn't understand why. 'I'm laughing at the stupidity of those who want change,' he said. 'No one can usurp His Majesty's power or kill him. He can only die of old age. Do you know why?' His eyes sought mine in the rear-view mirror. 'His Majesty wears a very powerful locket around his neck. There's a stone in it, blessed by Chinese sorcerers who live in the Tibetan mountains. No one can even touch His Majesty when he is wearing it. Even bullets cannot penetrate him. This magic locket has already saved him from three assassination attempts, two car accidents and one plane crash. These idiots know all this but still they want to waste their lives protesting.'

I thought he was joking at first. But no, he fully believed this. I learned later that this story is an article of faith among many of His Majesty's devotees in the City.

There were many other stories about His Majesty. One of the most popular ones was that for the last twenty years he had had blood cancer and every month he revitalized his blood with that of newborn children. That s why he was so strong and handsome.

Another story was that no one could guess in which of his seven palaces in the City he slept on any given night. Every day the servants would prepare a banquet in each one of those seven palaces. More than twenty-five women waited for him every night, naked, by his bedroom. If he arrived, he would take one of them inside. But the others couldn't leave. They had to wait till the morning in case he wanted one of them.

Amir chacha told me once that fathers waited in front of His Majesty's palaces with their virgin daughters. They considered it good fortune and a blessing if His Majesty picked their daughter for a night. It could change their lives completely. The reward for one night was a Mercedes car and 25,000 dinars.

These were not merely stories, but articles of faith. People also believed that His Majesty belonged to the Prophet's lineage and that was why Allah had given him this embarrassment of wealth and chosen him as their ruler. Amir chacha told me, on another occasion, that the palace had appointed people to spread such myths among the people.

His Majesty believed that power was his birthright and he has shown that he would go to any extent to keep it. He came to power by declaring that his father, who was abroad for medical treatment at the time, was not welcome to return. A brother who tried to usurp power is now languishing in some prison. Another brother is a drug addict who is just about semi-conscious most of the time. Two nephews who had resisted him were invited to the palace and shot dead.

There's even a story that His Majesty had a twin in his mother's womb. Knowing that the firstborn of each generation would inherit the kingship, the twins started arguing about who would emerge first from the womb. They did not heed their mother's scolding or warnings. The quarrel peaked as labour approached. When he realized that his twin would emerge first, His Majesty strangled him to death. The rest of his life is simply an extension of that first killing.

There are also funny stories about him. His Majesty liked fishing and would often take his boat to the middle of the sea for a few days. But his luck did not match his passion for fishing. Often, he wouldn't catch even a small fish to show for three days of fishing. He would take out his anger and humiliation on the boat workers. And so the workers found a solution. They would buy fish from other fishermen and keep them on the boat. When His Majesty started fishing, they would hook the fish on the rod and give it to him. His Majesty would happily pull it in from the sea.

So that was his fishing. Then there was hunting. His Majesty had heard all those legends about kings who went into the forest and brought home tigers and leopards. So he decided to get passionate about hunting. But would he find forests and tigers in this desert country? Instead, the Majesty had acres and acres of farms. Whenever the urge to hunt took over him, His Majesty would go out into the fields with his gun. His workers would release the hens and wild birds from their cages. His Majesty would chase them with his gun. After a bit of running, he would shoot one of those and bring it in, holding it by its wings. Then there would be a photo.

Though his workers were amused by these antics, they did not dare laugh. They would take the bird from him gravely and shower him with compliments as if he were a brave warrior who had hunted in a deep jungle.

I saw the subject of all these stories only once. One day, when I was waiting to cross the road, a police bike came by with its siren screaming and demanded that the cars in front stand to one side. I realized that some VIPs were coming. I waited around to see more. After three more bikes and a police car had passed, there was a convoy of cars and bikes. There were five luxury cars in the middle of that convoy and one of them contained His Majesty. I saw his face as if in a lightning strike. But I was not impressed. His Majesty was picking his nose.

Reward

The next day I was drinking coffee in the canteen when I heard loud laughter from the Arab staff's table. I joined them to find out what the joke was. That's the way I am made. I just have to know what's going on.

'So, what happened?' I asked.

Hasan whistled and muttered something under his breath. That was typical. If you asked him a serious question, his response would be a mocking whistle.

'What's the matter, Ali?' I asked Ali.

'Didn't you hear? The funniest thing in the world

108

happened in our country yesterday. Our rulers should be given an international prize for the Joke of the Year.'

I still didn't understand.

'Sameera, our government has announced a reward of one thousand dinars for every citizen of the country. What else is there to do but laugh? These idiots think that a thousand dinars will solve all our problems and we will withdraw our protests and live happily ever after. I feel ashamed at their stupidity.'

I didn't know what to say. I had heard this news yesterday. Taya mentioned it at dinner. Everyone who had a local passport was eligible and so my uncles, who held citizenship, talked about going to collect the money. But since baba was not a citizen, we were not eligible.

Even yesterday, I had wondered at the silliness of the stunt. Anyone could guess the motivation behind offering a 1000-dinar reward at a time when the neighbouring cities were in the throes of revolution and our own City was preparing to join them. What it revealed was not the government's affection for the people, but its cowardice.

Although everyone in the office mocked the reward, they all went to the municipality office to collect theirs. Over the next few days, new mobile phones and iPads and car accessories appeared. Not a single person declined the reward.

I joined the Malayalam Mafia in teasing the rewardees. 'So you'll protest against the government and then go and take these handouts? Such shamelessness!' Viju Prasad looked them in the face and asked, 'If you are protesting, protest properly. Be strong about refusing their bribes.'

'Why should we say no?' Hasan asked. 'This is a small portion of what we deserve. A tiny proportion of what they loot. Accepting this money does not mean we have reconciled with the government and would stop our protests. You just watch, our protests are going to get stronger. On 14 February, this country will finally understand the power of its youth.'

'Why 14 February? Isn't that the day of love?' I asked all of them. But no one had a good answer. So I googled and found out that 14 February was also the anniversary of many world events.

Iranian students captured the American embassy.

The bombings in Manila, the Philippines.

The death of Lebanese Prime Minister Rafi Harari in Hizbollah's attack.

The Fatwa against Salman Rushdie was declared on this day.

The revolution in Egypt began.

For the Arab youth, 14 February was not the day of love, it was the day of revolution.

A few days later, there was another incident that inflamed the young people of the country. 'This is the last straw,' Ali thundered. The previous night ambulances had screeched up and down the streets. Something was happening somewhere, and I felt the City's trepidation as I lay down to sleep. Baba was on night duty and he would know what was happening. But when I had got home, he was not there. Since the problems started, the government had increased the duty hours of all the police personnel. All leave had been cancelled and they could be called in to work at any time.

It was impossible to predict when each day's work would be done. All routines had disappeared.

As baba put it himself, in a few days he would have to make up for all the leisure of the past twenty years when he did not have to even shoo off a housefly.

I asked Ali what happened. But he ignored me. 'Ali, why are you annoyed with me? Am I sitting at the head of your government? Stop holding your breath and tell me what is going on.'

He relented. Last night the police had raided a wedding reception on the outskirts of the city and arrested several people for no reason. When some young men had resisted, the police used their weapons against them. Some of them were gravely injured. I found Ali's anger quite justified. Raiding a wedding reception is just too much. Anyone would be upset. But when baba came home he told me a different story. The wedding reception had been a front for a secret rebel meeting, he said, and the police had seized several weapons.

Who was right? Baba or Ali? I don't know. But something unprecedented was happening in this country. I didn't know what or who is behind it.

'The Government Is Ready for Negotiations' the newspaper headlines declared the next day.

Gardens

One day Ali and I got into an argument about the protests. I told him that my baba was a policeman and that he had never ever hit anyone, not even a criminal. After I had gone on for a bit, he became silent. 'Can I take you some place tonight after work?' he asked. I agreed.

We left after work in his car. Leaving the City behind, the car sped towards the villages. I had never visited those areas. I was a bit scared, partly because I was alone in the car with a man and partly because those villages did not seem to belong to this country. We were moving through narrow galis where black flags and banners flew and the walls were covered with slogans. I saw a woman writing on a wall with charcoal. Ali slowed the car down so I could read: 'If the men do not go out to fight against this unjust regime, women will do it.'

Ali parked the car in front of the wooden gate of an old house. I stepped out reluctantly. I felt as if snakes were crawling around my feet. Why had I stubbornly set out with Ali?

The house was made of limestone and palm tree fronds. An old man was sitting on a chair in the veranda, fanning himself with an old palm leaf. Ali went up to him and kissed his hand and they exchanged loving greetings. The old man looked at me curiously. Ali introduced me. 'Why do you look so terrified?' the old man asked me. 'Think of this as your own house and come inside.' Upon hearing this, all my feelings of strangeness melted away. His English was mesmerizing. I have rarely heard Arabs speak such good English.

'He is my uncle. He was a schoolteacher,' Ali said. Then he told his uncle about our argument and that my baba was a policeman. When Ali finished, his uncle laughed as if he had heard a joke.

112

'This country is a giant jail with many beautiful gardens,' he said once he was done laughing. 'The workers in the jail only see the gardens, so they don't know what a harsh place this is. But the prisoners know. That is the difference between us and you, my daughter. As far as you are concerned, the police are good people, harmless men doing their job. But that is not my experience. That is why Ali brought you here.

'One day I was on my way back from school. It was an evening in 1981. A police vehicle stopped me on the way and asked me to get in. Of course I asked them why. They insisted I should get in. When I refused to do so without any justification, three policemen came out and forced me to get in.

'They made me wait in the police station for six hours for no reason. I was not even allowed to sit, I had to stand for all those hours. Then a policeman came up to me and started hitting me as he said, how dare you not get into the police car when we ask you to. I thought maybe they would let me go after that. But they kept me for days, torturing me. They wanted me to confess that I had conspired against the government. Or I must point out people who had. It's true that I have spoken openly against the government and have participated in protests. But I had never conspired to overthrow the government. My conscience did not let me confess to a crime I had never committed or point fingers at innocents.

'They hit me with their batons and guns. They applied electric shocks to my genitals. They hung me upside down for hours. They forced me to drink dirty water and chemicals.

113

They made me stand on a block of ice. For three years, I journeyed on roads of torture. When they saw that my spirit was still unvanquished, they moved me to a dark cell. I don't know if you will believe me, but they left me there, without any trial, not for one or two years, but for a long eighteen years. My youth was eaten away by those eighteen years in jail.'

He paused for a few moments. Only the fan kept moving. Then his words started moving again with the fan.

'For most of my time in jail, I was in a secret prison under a huge auditorium in the middle of the city. Except for a few senior police officers, no one even knew of this prison's existence. The cell was only as long as my body. I could not stand upright in it. I lay on the bare floor. During the first twelve years, I never saw any sunlight or sky. Like a corpse, I had no connection to the outside world. There was a small opening in the wall through which they gave me food. A hole in the ground in the same room was my toilet. I had to sleep next to it. There was a tap next to the hole for washing and bathing. No soap, no brush, no toothpaste, not even a candle for some light. In those eighteen years, I changed my clothing only twice. And for eighteen years, I ate the exact same meal three times a day – two kuboos, some curd. There were other cells near mine. Some prisoners were sick. They died in those cells. For days their corpses lay there. I can still smell all that rotting flesh.

'At night, if I strained my ears in my underground cell, I could hear the sounds of music and theatre above. People were celebrating life, dancing happily, with no idea that some innocents were rotting below, a few feet under them.

114

Think about it, I am not talking of medieval autocrats or the Mughals or Ottomans. I am talking of your own times, about the city that so many call heaven on earth. Thousands have sacrificed their lives for the freedom in this city; perhaps you wonder why we keep throwing our lives away. I could have easily escaped my cell if I had confessed to some crime or betrayed some innocents. But my self-respect was too precious to me.

'There's a story I heard in my childhood. Before the communists came to power in Russia, one day a group of the tsar's soldiers captured some young communists and whipped them. The soldiers stood in a line in a field and the prisoners had to walk in front of them, getting whipped by each soldier. After getting whipped by three or four soldiers, even the strongest of the men would fall to the ground. One young man, picked up a blade of grass from the ground and placed it between his teeth before his turn began. He walked past the soldiers and took the whipping. He reached the other end of the line and took out the grass from his mouth. It did not even have a tooth mark on it. To the shocked soldiers, the young man said, "I am a communist. My name is Stalin."

'I cannot even begin to tell you how inspired we were by this story. Lying in my dark cell I would remember Stalin. The Iranian revolution of 1978 did not cause any ripples in my generation. Even when the world praised it as a democratic revolution, we knew it was but a theocratic revolution. I believed then and continue to believe that Islam cannot overtake communism. But just as communists were hunted everywhere in the world when I was a young man, today Muslims are hunted everywhere. And so I see in Islam the strength of an animal that is preyed upon. And my spirit is with them.

'See this fan? When I went to jail, there was no air conditioning here. This was what I used then. My children kept this fan for me, for eighteen years. Today, this house is air-conditioned. No fans are needed. But I cannot do without it. It is as if my hands are fused to it. And communism is also like that. I know it is too old-fashioned for your generation. But I need its breeze.

'It was in 1999 when I was released from prison that I heard that the USSR had disintegrated. I couldn't have even imagined it before. I got another piece of bad news when I came home. My beloved eldest daughter Fatima had died when I was in jail. If you ask me which news shattered me more, the honest answer is: the disintegration of communist Russia.

As he finished speaking, tears rolled down my cheeks. I held his hand as we said our goodbyes. We were silent on our ride back. After a while, Ali said, 'Remember you asked me once why I never come to any concerts even though I love playing the guitar? Sameera, my guitar is for playing my sorrows, not my joys. My guitar is for the songs of the abandoned and oppressed. After my uncle came back from jail, I simply could not go to any more music shows. You invited me to a Justin Bieber concert once. Even though you insisted, I refused to come. Whenever I see a stage where music or dance is performed, I feel a shiver of fear. For how many years my mamu lay under a stage like that . . . Who knows, maybe my baba is still lying somewhere

116

under a stage. How can I stand on top of all that terror to sing and dance?'

The Return

Mishumi was returning – the news spread through the city like a welcome wind. Mishumi was one of the first leaders to criticize His Majesty's administration. It was he who had led the revolt of 1992. But the government had ruthlessly stamped down that revolt and exiled Mishumi. For twenty years he had lived in London as a political refugee. His Majesty didn't permit Mishumi to set foot in the country after that. Mishumi had asked to return when his mother and then his wife and nine-year-old daughter Farah died. That did not happen. Even when he was in London, Mishumi had supported and steered protest movements in this country. But no one had expected him to return. Now the government had become too weak to resist his return. It could only look on helplessly as the people of the country, like wild birds rising from sand dunes, took to the streets.

History was repeating itself in Mishumi's return, people said. Years ago, Ayatollah Khomeini too had returned to Iran after fifteen years of exile, to overthrow the Shah's regime and lead the Islamic revolution to victory. Mishumi too, the people hoped, would become their saviour. They gathered in the airport as soon as they heard that he had reached Cairo. It took him two more days to reach the City. They waited patiently for him. As soon as he landed, all the roads in the city led to the airport. A crowd of more

117

than ten lakh people waited for him at the airport. But Mishumi surprised them and the assembled journalists by leaving the airport without a single word to them. The crowd followed him. From the airport he went straight to the grave of his daughter. There, where a nine-year-old life had been reduced to a mound of sand, he placed a handful of flowers. Then he broke his silence with a single sentence, 'Freedom first, then negotiations.'

Freedom

The protests had been faraway events till then. I only had hearsay knowledge about how big they were or how loud the protesters were. But that Friday, the protest began at the junction near our house. People started flowing into the city, from around three in the afternoon. There were men and women, old and young, even children. Some held the national flag and others held the white flag of peace. Yet others had draped the national flag around themselves – they called out that this country belonged to them, not to anyone else. As more and more people joined the crowds, they sat down on the streets waiting for the protests to begin. Others found a place in the park in front of our house. The leaders of the protest arrived soon after. Loudspeakers attached to poles appeared along the length of the street. For at least five kilometres, there were microphones every hundred metres. By four in the afternoon, the highway was an ocean of black and white. From my balcony, I could see people as far as the eye could see. All the women of our household crowded into the balcony with me and all the men, except taya, took their places on the terrace. Taya stayed in his room, as if nothing was happening outside. The roofs around us were crowded with spectators. Vehicles could barely move in the road below. Volunteers ran around trying to make place for the occasional vehicle. I wondered how all these people had got here, where were their cars parked? There wasn't a single policeman to be seen.

For foreigners like us, who came from countries where demonstrations and strikes were an everyday event, the protest was not a new sight. But we had never seen something like this here in this adopted country. Even two weeks ago we could not have imagined such a crowd taking over that highway. We were even wonderstruck that the place could hold so many people.

I called Ali to see if he was nearby. He replied that he had arrived an hour ago and that he could see me on my balcony. But I could not see him in the crowd. 'I am going mad with excitement seeing this crowd. Can I come to your balcony and take a video?' he asked. I stopped him. 'Certainly not. The next thing you know my family would start yelling at me again.'

The protests began at five. At the front of the march was a banner with the word 'FREEDOM'. Mishumi and other leaders and religious figures were arrayed behind the banner. There were three life-size photos behind them, of Nelson Mandela, Mahatma Gandhi and Riad al-Turk. The first two are of course famous around the world. But perhaps not many know of Riad al-Turk outside the Arab world. I didn't know either. It was Ali who told me the next day.

Riad al-Turk is Syria's Mandela. He was imprisoned for as long as Mandela had been. He was not a terrorist and he did not conspire to overthrow the government. The accusation against him was that he had controversial opinions, led demonstrations and was a member of a political party. Like many others in the Arab world, he spent many years in jail. But he was indefatigable. I read later that he declared himself willing to spend another eighteen years in prison protesting against the dictatorship.

The three photos at the protest meant a big change. In earlier days, Shia protests had been full of pictures of various imams in the Prophet's lineage, Ayatollah Khomeini, Nasrallah, black flags and Prophetic verses. But with these three photos and the white flags and national flags, they were sending the administration a powerful message that what they wanted was peace, not conflict. That power was evident in their slogans, their placards, their songs, their raised fists.

With men on one side and women on the other side of the road, the protesters moved forward. It was as if a black river and a white river were flowing next to each other. The flags, in red and white, were like waves in those rivers. A few protesters held signs that were more provocative. For instance, one placard showed photos of two rulers who had recently been overthrown in other countries and a third photo of His Majesty with a huge question mark on it.

120

I still remember the sign held up by a small girl. It said, 'Enough Humiliation, Enough Injustice, Enough Discrimination, Enough Majesty, Enough.' Other protesters had similar messages.

'No more Sunnis, No more Shias, Only Human Beings in this Country.'

'The Invader Must Leave, Return the Country to its People.'

'We Will Defend Our Rights with the Last Drop of Blood.'

'Forty Years of Dictatorship, But Not Even Four More Days.'

A huge group of journalists including foreign correspondents and photographers and videographers were moving alongside the protesters to capture the news.

We heard a snort behind us and turned around to see that taya was with us. We had thought he was in his room, not interested in the protests.

'Look how eager the women are to get rid of His Majesty,' he said. 'The poor things have no idea they can protest so vigorously only because His Majesty's administration has protected their freedom as women. They can go to school, college, work. If they want to go to a party at night, they can do so. They can wear whatever clothes they want. And they can protest alongside men, if that's what they want. Who can stop them? But if His Majesty's government were to fall, that very minute all these freedoms will be curtailed. The first thing the next government will do is lock up women in their homes, as if they were wild pigs. The very people they mobilized into power will end all their freedoms. That is the grand finale of every Islamic revolution. When will these women understand? Yes, protest away. After all, the leg can stretch out only as far as the blanket will let it . . .'

He walked away angrily and we resumed watching the protest. At some point, police helicopters appeared in the sky. The person who was calling out slogans through the microphone stopped and said something else. For a moment, the City was drowned in the laughter of five lakh people. It was as if their scorn had scaled a summit. If His Majesty had heard that laugh I think he would have committed suicide. Death is a better fate for a ruler than being mocked by his people.

I have witnessed any number of marches and demonstrations in my country. But I have never seen such an orderly protest – not one person was idle. Everyone was chanting slogans. There was no elbowing or shoving. The demonstration maintained its order till the end, till the very last row of protesters had left. Behind them came a row of volunteers who were cleaning up after the demonstrators, picking up napkins and empty water bottles. When the protesters were gone, the streets were cleaner than before.

That was how it was when Shias led protests. The discipline they had learned from their rites and rituals was evident in the way they protested. They chanted sad songs rather than offensive slogans. Like children in a classroom, the protesters remained calm and tidy. It was as if even while protesting, they would not forgo discipline.

The march went all the way to the Square of Pearls, one of the most important spaces in the City. Political and religious leaders addressed the crowd. Their chief message was that the protests would continue till His Majesty stepped down. A girl studying in the tenth standard recited her poem, titled 'His Majesty'.

Hey old man
Self-proclaimed Protector of Justice
Listen to me.

Even if I forgave you
For all you have done so far
You would still brand us traitors
You would punish us with death

Listen to me, evil one
Listen to the demand of the people
Leave!
Take your majesty with you
Leave the country behind

Listen to me, you torturer
Where do you find the strength for your hypocrisy?
You oppress everyone
Women, children, men
Then you invite us to negotiate?

No, No, No.
Just one word for you: No
We only have one demand
Return our country to us
This land is ours

The crowd applauded non-stop for at least five minutes. Then the leaders declared that the era of weekend protests was over. The protests would be constant and endless till His Majesty stepped down.

Part 4

Weekend God

Protest Camps

The government and the police expected the protesters to leave after their march. But instead they camped in the Square of Pearls. People were doing this in other cities where the protests were going strong. The police had not foreseen this and were powerless to stop it. They, including taya, had been too busy laughing at the youth and dismissing their plans. But within hours, hundreds of camps came up in the Square. Clearly, the protesters had planned very methodically – they knew where each camp should go up. There were separate camps for journalists, for the medical team, for artists, for young women, for students, for housewives, even for different villages. Within a night, they had everything they needed to camp indefinitely – generators, water tanks, portable toilets, benches, chairs, couches, tables, microphones, Internet facilities, TVs, dish antennae, rice, bread, juice.

On the flyover next to the Square of Pearls, the protesters hung huge banners that said, 'His Majesty Must Resign, His Majesty Must Go on Trial, and End Injustice'. Other posters were more incendiary and had pictures of His Majesty standing in front of a noose or being whipped or tied to a cannon.

Till a few days ago, no one could have imagined such things happening in this country. The public had become used to living inside a circle of fear. They were a nursery-school public that was afraid to mention His Majesty without reciting a long string of honorifics first. Afraid of playing songs too loudly in their homes. Afraid of honking unnecessarily on the road. Afraid of spitting outside. Afraid of throwing a piece of paper on the street. In a few days, all those fears that had been stagnant for so long suddenly drained away.

In the past, even a few words of graffiti against His Majesty would have been erased quickly by the police. But now they could do nothing to the protesters in the Square. Perhaps they knew that the crowd was in a do-or-die mood, and were wary. So the police did not even look in that direction. The protesters themselves redirected the traffic. 'What brave policemen!' I teased baba. 'As soon as they saw a few protesters, they ran into their holes.'

The next day onwards, like a river flowing to the sea, people from the villages started pouring into the Square of Pearls. Each village was organized into its own group, like pilgrims. Many other groups passed before our eyes on the highway, including students from different universities; doctors, nurses and paramedics and workers' organizations, all holding up banners identifying themselves, shouting slogans against His Majesty and praising the protesters.

I was jealous of them. They were all so full of hope and

128

excitement. When they met on the street, they greeted each other affectionately and wished each other good luck. At work, they talked about meeting at the Square in the evening. It was as if a sleeping people had suddenly woken up. They were fully confident of their success.

One day when I was standing on the balcony watching, I saw a middle-aged man walk into the Square of Pearls with his son on his shoulders. The boy had a national flag in his hands. While the other protesters were in groups, the father was by himself, calling out slogans against the administration. Then he caught sight of me on the balcony. He must have guessed that I was a foreigner. Pointing his finger at me, he said, 'Get ready to leave this country. The end is coming for you and your kind. If not in my time, at least in my son's.' I tried to move out of his vision but he fixed his eyes on me and went on, partly to me, partly to society itself. 'Do you know why I have lifted him on to my shoulders? I want him to see the world from a height I cannot. I want him to understand the injustice that goes on in this country. You shameless foreigners, you are dogs eating the leftovers of this government. Till you leave, this country will not get better.'

He was not alone in his opinion. Many protesters felt that foreigners like us were the reason they were denied equality, justice and employment opportunities. Even Ali commented from time to time that it was the foreign workers that made the government so arrogant. 'They know that they can run the country without us. That's why so many protests have failed. So the foreigners must go for the government to fall.' The Malayalam Mafia tried to counter Ali's argument. 'We

129

are not taking away your income. We are working for a very meagre pay compared to what you would make.'

To that Ali said, 'The reason we never get these jobs is because you are ready to work for such meagre pay. If you were not here, one of us would be paid well to do the same job.'

'But why should they pay you more? Why can't you work for the same salary as we do? Why do you need more?'

'But why are you comparing your lifestyle with ours? There's a difference in our circumstances. This is a rich country that makes huge profits from its oil investments. Why should the people of this country live like the citizens of India, where millions live below the poverty line? There's a difference between being poor in a rich country and being poor in a poor country.'

The arguments went on in an endless loop. There were no real answers to these questions.

There was another incident I should tell you about, Javed. One day I went out with Sippy auntie in her car. We were waiting for the lights to change at a signal when a bus stopped next to us. I looked inside the bus aimlessly. A woman was staring at me angrily. I had to turn my face away, unable to take the intensity of her gaze. It was as if her eyes were burning me with all the resentment I had sensed in Ali and Ahmed and Yunus and the protester with his son on his shoulders. It was not merely resentment, it was a mix of envy, self-pity, helplessness and desperation. Her eyes were saying, 'Look at you, travelling in a fancy car, getting rich in my own country, while I have to take this service bus in this heat. You are responsible for my misery.' I could not face her. I realize now that I began feeling guilty then. I had indeed played a part in making their lives unhappy. After that, I avoided travelling in the car with Sippy auntie and other family members. Not only that, every day when I was about to eat, I looked at my meal and prayed, this food is not my food. It is stolen from the people of this country. It is flavoured with injustice. All-merciful God, please forgive me for this theft.

Death Market

When the protests began, foreigners like us looked on the Square of Pearls with fear and hatred, as if it were a kind of hell. We worried that we might accidentally stray there and become objects of police surveillance. Amir chacha told me one day that the camps were full of CIDs and that every movement in the camps was being observed. People were afraid of anything that involved the Shias. Baba told me that people were scared of even watching their mourning processions with their chest-beating and sad songs. There were rumours in the City that the police took photos of everyone at the procession as well as those who had been watching, and kept them under observation. And so, to us, the Square of Pearls was like a terrorist den. We looked at Viju Prasad with awe when he went there and came back alive with news of the protesters.

But Ali, Hasan and Muneer Gazi kept inviting us there. 'Our protests are not against foreigners, they are against the administration. Our camps are open to anyone who wants to support us. You are welcome to visit us.' As the days passed, our fears slowly evaporated. As the City rapidly descended into anarchy, we wondered who should be scared of whom. After I heard that two of my uncles had passed by the camps and that the protesters had welcomed them with juice, I itched to visit the camps myself. I proposed the idea in Cattle Class and it was accepted. And so one day after work, we returned via the Square of Pearls. We saw the flags, the banners and the tents. But maybe because it was only afternoon, there weren't too many people. A few people were crowded in front of the food counter. Others were drinking coffee and chatting. Most tents were empty. We were like disappointed children who had gone to the zoo but did not see the lion. All that we had accomplished was that the car spent a lot more time in traffic.

But when I secretly told Aisha auntie about my visit, she got very excited. 'Sameera, I have never seen a protest camp except on TV. Please, please, please take me there,' she begged like a child.

Of course Taya Ghar had declared the protest camp to be the vilest place on earth. Sippy auntie practically tore to pieces the two uncles who had visited the camp last week. 'We are a police family. We eat His Majesty's rice. How can we not be loyal to him? I don't want anyone going to see that pigsty,' she commanded from the common living room.

But I decided to flout her orders and take Aisha auntie to the camp. One evening, I asked her to come out with me. We told everyone at Taya Ghar that we were going to the souk. 'Do you have to go out during such troubled times?' Sippy auntie grumbled but we shrugged it off. When

Farhana asked to come with us, we discouraged her. We even wore our purdahs so no one would recognize us in the camp. Luckily purdah has some good uses.

We walked on to the streets and melted into a big group of protesters. It was fun walking with them. We even shouted a few slogans. I looked over at Aisha auntie and saw the laughter in her eyes. The camp itself felt like a carnival. It was a very different place from what it was during my previous visit. All the tents were overflowing with people. There was eating, drinking, sloganeering and street theatre, concerts and dice games.

A mullah was making a speech some distance away. He was speaking in English, perhaps because there were foreign TV channels recording the speech. We listened for a bit. It was a passionate speech.

'My beloved people, who needs a protest full of white flags? To put an end to His Majesty's rule, what we need is a death protest. Our circumstances demand nothing less. My young friends, this is Allah's war. He will forgive all the sins of anyone who loses his life in this war. This is certain. Heaven will become your home. This is certain. At the door to heaven, Imam Hassan will be waiting to usher you in. Seventy-two houris will be waiting for you. This is certain. You can enjoy them for eternity. This is certain. What else do you want? Get ready for death.'

Death, death, death. He kept repeating that word. We were terrified. Had Allah declared war? Did the Prophet promise such things? Then why was he so certain? Who was he to promise all this?

Our lives suddenly seemed in danger. Slowly Aisha

auntie and I backed out of the audience. We sneaked out of the camp when no one was looking. We didn't just walk home, we were running for our lives. Only after we got home did we breathe easy. Even then the words kept ringing in our ears. Death, death, death.

Mock Parliament

'Today is our election day,' Laila declared one day as soon as she walked into the office.

'Elections?' We gaped.

'Who cares what His Majesty and his cronies do. Let them go to hell. Today we are going to elect our prime minister and other important ministers. The elections will be held from four to eight and the results will be declared tonight.'

I thought of it as a joke, like when children play mock parliament. What was the point of people pretending to hold elections in a country that had its own government, police and army? They might as well play football without a ball.

But it was not a joke for those who participated in that election. There were three candidates for prime minister, including Mishumi. One of them was from Ali's village. Ali campaigned for him all day in the studio. But Hasan bet that Mishumi would win by a huge majority. He would destroy all the other candidates with his charisma. He campaigned for Mishumi. Ali and he even got into an argument about it in the canteen.

In the evening, people started flowing into the Square of Pearls. That's when I realized this was serious business for them. People from every single village participated in the elections. There were special booths for each village. Those who voted were marked as attending and those who did not vote were also noted.

Even before the elections, there had been an attendance register for each village at the protest camp. There were designated groups in each village to 'persuade' those who hesitated to join the protests at the Square of Pearls. No one could stay away from the protests. And if anyone did, they were isolated in their villages.

On election day, attendance was compulsory. After all, the protesters decided, democracy was a public process. So every member of the public must participate in this public process. It was crucial, Ali said, to show His Majesty how to conduct an election in this county where there had never been one.

With Mishumi up for the post of prime minister, the elections were bound to cause a stir. The other candidates were all important industrialists, political leaders, lawyers, journalists and human rights activists.

As expected, Mishumi won by a huge majority. We heard later that the announcement was greeted with a long round of applause by the large crowds that had waited well past midnight in the Square of Pearls. Abdullah Hala, a well-known industrialist and one of the main organizers of the protest, was elected as the assistant prime minister and the lawyer Khalid Qudair was to be the home minister. I do not remember the others now.

The next day the newspapers were full of headlines such as 'His Majesty's Era is Over' and 'The People have Elected the Prime Minister of their Choice'. But our radio stations still kept playing music.

Condom Revolutionaries

I often heard jokes about the protesters in our Cattle Class conversations. The Malayalam Mafia came up with names that poked fun at the protesters. 'Part-time Revolutionaries' were ones like Ali who went to work during the day and went to the camps in the evenings. Then there were 'Sandwich Revolutionaries' who signed in to work in the morning and went straight to the camp for breakfast. 'Biriyani Revolutionaries' were those who turned up in the camps at lunchtime. It wasn't the Malayalam Mafia who made up those names. They were only repeating jokes that were circulating in the City.

But while these were jokes, one day I heard a serious allegation. It was Yunus who mentioned it in Cattle Class. There was a new class of protesters called 'Condom Revolutionaries'. He said that in the name of protesting, a lot of immoral activities were going on in the camps. Many of the young women who were ostensibly protesting were simply there to hang out in their boyfriends' cars. You couldn't walk into the camps without stepping on condoms, he said. The tents had turned into brothels. To prove his point, Yunus showed us a pro-government newspaper that had published a giant picture of a carelessly discarded condom. All the foreign channels including BBC and CNN had published this news.

But the leaders of the protest dismissed it. When someone raised the matter in a press conference, this is what they said. 'Friends, this is a protest full of celebrations. Three or four pairs of young people have got married here in this protest camp. Others have got engaged. Yet others are celebrating their anniversary here. There are parents who want to hold birthday parties for their children here. We are not against any of this. We don't want this to be a protest full of sanctions and punishments. That is the old-fashioned way of protesting. But protests can be different. This is a protest that emerged from our common humanity. Anything human is welcome here.

'We are not afraid of human nature. And so we are not going to be shocked or ashamed simply because a condom was found here. That condom may well have been placed here by some lapdog from the administration or by a religious fanatic who could not bear to see women participating fully in this protest. But so what if it was indeed a protester's condom? So what if two lovers want to protest by celebrating their bodies? This is not a monastic protest. This is not a protest for lifeless statues. This is a protest for ordinary people, human beings with bodies and needs. That's what makes it a human protest.

'Look, I don't even know who is sitting next to me. We are simply people who came from many different directions and united for a cause. We don't have a centralized leadership. But like the different spokes of a wheel, we are moving towards a common aim. To understand the nature of this protest, you have to set aside your old-fashioned views. Wasn't it a leader of yours who said, 'Never mind whether the cat is black or white, what matters is that it catches the mouse'? We don't care about the colour of the cat, its size or its shape. But one thing is certain. This cat will catch the mouse.'

The National Bird

During the day, the City was quiet. People went to work, traffic ran smoothly, offices worked as usual. There was not even a hint of the trouble in the country. By afternoon the atmosphere would change. Two sounds would fill the air, heralding this transformation – the sound of ambulances screeching on the streets and that of helicopters circling in the sky. When we heard these sounds, we knew that trouble was brewing somewhere. Fear would fill our hearts. We would worry about getting home, wonder if something would happen on the way back, pray that there were no traffic jams. Those who were at home wondered if those who had gone out to work were safe and those who had gone out to work wondered if those at home were safe. So once it became afternoon, no work was possible. Hasan would find some excuse to leave. The rest of us would gather to gossip about the previous day's march or how a foreigner was beaten up in the street last week. Who knew or cared whether these stories were real or exaggerations. But still, everyone had a story of their own.

Once the helicopters became an everyday sight and

sound, the jokers in the Malayalam Mafia gave it a nickname: national bird. Quickly the name became popular in our office. Ali and Hasan especially enjoyed that name. Whenever we heard the sound of the copter, Ali would comment, 'Oh, the national bird is out on its rounds. We can all go home.' Cue group laughter in the studio.

Soon enough, the name became popular even outside our office. You only had to mention 'the national bird' and people immediately knew what you were talking about. Even taya and baba, who were devoted to the government and quick to reprimand any anti-police talk, couldn't help laughing when they heard that name.

Another sound then joined the cacophony of afternoon sounds. It was a kind of rhythmic honking.

Pee Pee Pippippi

Pee Pee Pippippi

Pee Pee Pippippi

Hundreds of cars would honk in exactly this pattern as they drove on the highway. This, in a country where it was illegal to honk unnecessarily. I assumed that they were honking simply for the pleasure of flouting that law.

One day at home I said to baba, 'I wish they would stop this horrible noise.'

'Do you know what they mean by this noise?' Baba asked me.

Neither Ali nor Hasan nor Yunus had said anything to me.

'What they are saying is "Down, Down, Majesty".'

That's when I realized that the rhythm had its own meaning.

Pee Pee Pippippi
Down, Down, Majesty
Pee Pee Pippippi
Down, Down, Majesty

Whoever thought that up? I was wonderstruck at their ingenuity and said so.

'Don't think this is your Ali's and Hasan's work. This is not child's play. There are major powers at work here. And that's the kind of intelligence that is working behind the scenes,' baba said.

I chalked this down to baba's suspicious police mind.

Together, the sounds of the ambulances, the helicopters and the honking cars created an atmosphere of constant emergency. This wasn't just my imagination. The country was, in fact, beginning to move into a state of emergency and instability.

The Neros of Orange Radio

One day when I was hosting a live show, Rajeevan sir, our managing director, came into the studio. He was with a renowned journalist, one who was rumoured to be one of the silent partners of Broadway Communications. Rajeevan sir never came to the studio or interrupted programmes. Once in a while he would accompany some important guest to the studio to interview them. But we always got advance notice before this happened. So when he suddenly walked into my studio, I was surprised. Kapil bhai came to the intercom and asked me to come out. I wrapped up what I was saying and went to the switch room.

'Rajeevan sir needs to make a public statement as soon as possible. After this song, announce that you are making way for an emergency message.'

I did as I was told. Rajeevan sir went live and read out his prepared statement.

'Dear brothers and sisters, I am Rajeevan. I am the managing director of your beloved radio stations Tunes Malayalam and Radio Orange. I am taking over the microphone to share some important thoughts.

'As we all know, this adopted land of ours is going through a dangerous time. Anarchic forces have poked their heads out, like snakes in a desert, to hiss at our beloved Majesty, who protects us and takes care of us. These protesters want to extinguish the harmony of this country, destroy its economy and humiliate our country internationally. Clearly, there are secret forces behind them.

'It is our duty to prove without doubt that we stand with His Majesty who has nurtured us like his own children. And now we have an opportunity to show our undying devotion to him. This coming Friday, there will be a huge rally in support of His Majesty after Friday prayers at the Grand Mosque. I humbly request every foreigner who is loyal to His Majesty to attend that rally. None of you must hesitate. We should participate in this rally as if it were our own family matter. We should express our love for His Majesty and this country. Let's not see this as a problem happening in someone else's country. This is after all a question of our own survival here. This Friday we will show this country that we are united in our love for His Majesty. In the hope that the country will return to normalcy soon, I, Rajeevan, will now sign off.'

Next the journalist spoke. He said similar things. 'We are foreigners here. We may not be interested in the politics of the country. But this is an opportunity to show our loyalty to His Majesty and this country. We must rise to the occasion.'

They left after instructing Imthiaz sir and Viju Prasad to start airing an exciting promo for the rally. Imthiaz sir and I prepared the Hindi promo. 'This Friday, let's gift our hearts to this country,' it said. Shahbaz set it to a tune. The Malayalam Mafia also made a similar promo. All week, we sent those promos out every ten minutes to fly through the airwaves.

Ass-Lickers' Rally

I had no desire to participate in the Friday rally. In Cattle Class, we had often discussed whose side to take if push came to shove. We had decided that both sides looked equally strong and that the best thing to do was to keep a neutral stance so that whoever won, our position would not be affected. So I was loath to attend the rally. But taya insisted that everyone in the house must go. Even stubborn Sippy auntie could not disobey this edict. So I went, if half-heartedly.

The rally at the Grand Mosque was a much bigger performance than the protesters on the highway in front of us. Lakhs of people turned up, including lots of foreigners from India, Bangladesh and Pakistan. Most of them were poor labourers who had been trucked in from labour camps. And then others like us, who had to prove our loyalty. Rajeevan sir was in the front row of the rally. It had been rumoured in the City that everyone who participated in the rally would get a ten-dinar reward. Many of the attendees were hoping for the reward.

In imitation of the protesters, the Friday rally also held up white flags of peace and the national flag. There were also banners proclaiming the goodness of His Majesty. The foreign minister inaugurated the rally. What other proof did we need to know that the rally was government sponsored? 'Look how much the people of this country love His Majesty!' he told the foreign correspondents.

After about three hours of this, all the women of our family returned home in Sippy auntie's car. But taya and the men stayed till the very end of the rally. After all they had high stakes in His Majesty's survival, perhaps even more than His Majesty himself. Their lives were inextricably tied to his administration.

It was only the next day when I arrived in the studio that I understood the kind of emotional turmoil caused by the rally. The Arab staff refused to talk to us. They were angry that we had attended the rally. Their attitude was, 'How is this any of your business? You are outsiders and this is an internal matter. History will not forgive you.'

Around the City, foreigners were hearing similar reactions. Even other foreigners criticized the studio for

Rajeevan sir's public message and the rally promos. 'In one day, you have made locals into our enemies by interfering unnecessarily,' they emailed and texted.

Ali gave me a dark look when he saw me. 'So you went to the ass-lickers' rally?' I had never heard such sarcasm from him before. I had no answer for him.

'He knew he would never get a single local to support him, so he had to round up all the foreigners,' Ali went on. 'Stupid man. He is desperate to win. But you? You betrayed the aspirations of this country for your own selfish interests. Sameera, you of all people know very well why we are protesting. When I think about how even you attended his rally, I just lose my faith in humanity.'

'Ali, please.' I started crying. 'You have no idea how helpless I am. The women in our house don't have as much freedom as your women do. I have my limits.'

But he refused to understand. He went away without waiting to hear any more.

That night, his Facebook status was, 'History will judge you. These streets will not forgive you.'

Ruin

Even amidst protests, the String Walkers kept meeting for musical evenings. But one day during a jam session, Ali started playing 'Hawk of Lebanon' on his guitar. As soon as he began, Salman jumped up and yelled, 'Stop that stupid song.' There had never been such an interruption in a String Walkers session. Each person had the right to sing or play whatever song they wanted. For a few moments, Ali was paralysed with shock. Then he came around.

'I have the freedom to play whatever I want,' he said.

'Look Ali, we know what is going on in this country. But we have never brought politics into our music. That's what you are doing by playing this song. I am not going to simply stand by and let you do that,' Salman said.

'This song has nothing to do with what is going on in the country. It is about a hawk in Lebanon.'

'Are you mocking us now? Even small children know who the hawk is and what his organization does. You don't have to explain.'

'Why shouldn't I explain? Do any of the Arab countries who eat and drink money do anything against Israeli colonialism except occasional vocal exercises? There is only one organization fighting to uphold the Arab people's pride. Hizbollah and Nasrallah deserve this song.'

'Don't talk to me about Hizbollah. When the Israeli army marched into Lebanon the first time, they greeted the soldiers with rose water and rice. It was only later that they turned hostile to Israel. When they couldn't get power for themselves.'

'Please, let's stop this conversation right here,' Ifran said. 'This is a never-ending argument. We can believe what we want. Let's not bring those beliefs to String Walkers.'

'Okay, I am done,' Salman said. 'But Ali cannot play that song here.'

Of course that made Ali even more stubborn. 'I don't know why that song is so humiliating to you. If I am playing anything today, it will be that song.'

'I am not going to sit around listening to some terrorist anthem. I am leaving right now.' Salman left, dragging Nazar with him. After a few minutes, Farah followed them silently.

Ali also took his guitar and left after a bit. That left me, Ifran, Roger and Sophia. We were silent. There was nothing to say. We had believed that even as the country fell to pieces around us, even as communities broke down, music would keep our little band strong and tight, like a taut string on a guitar. But even our miniature world was in ruins now.

Cholera

It was a small incident, perhaps deliberate, perhaps accidental, that marked the turn of the protest into a sectarian conflict. A young woman drove her car through the Square of Pearls. She had pasted a picture of His Majesty on the rear window. This had become a thing, since the protests started, with His Majesty's supporters pasting his picture on their cars to show their support. Protesters stopped her car and asked her to remove the picture before proceeding through the Square. The woman not only refused but also insulted the protesters. An argument followed, and she moved her car forward, driving over the feet of a few protesters. The angry protesters tried to attack the car. But somehow she drove through them, and got out of the Square. Some of the young men from the Square followed her and though they didn't capture her, they found out where she lived. They tried to attack her house in the night. She lived in a Sunni area and the villagers there were expecting such an attack and had organized themselves to guard her house. They surrounded the attackers and nearly beat them to death. At dawn, their half-dead bodies were dropped off at a hospital.

The news took the City by storm. The Sunnis heard that Shia youth had attacked a Sunni village. The Shias heard that the Sunnis had almost killed a few young Shia men. Like cholera, the news spread from village to village. Sunnis in Shia-dominated areas and Shias in Sunni-dominated areas were under attack. The police were more concerned with saving their own lives than controlling the violence.

Like a buzzing mosquito, fear started circling the City. Anyone could be attacked anywhere. People started constructing barricades and checkposts at the entrances of their galis and villages. They took turns guarding those entrances. Strangers had to show their identity cards. Anyone deemed suspicious was stopped and beaten up.

One night we were having dinner at home when Khalid chacha came running inside. He locked the door behind him. He was trembling and panting. We were startled and immediately surrounded him. He told us that a gang of young men were a few houses away, attacking people on the street, shutting down shops and forcing open the doors of houses. Chacha's head was bleeding but he refused to tell us what had happened. Only when taya insisted did he tell us that the young men had hit him. They were protesters taking revenge on foreigners for supporting His Majesty at the Friday rally.

All the Pakistanis in our street assembled that night in

Taya Ghar. We smelled fear on each other. We had to do something or they would not let us live in peace, it was decided. Someone suggested putting up a checkpost like in other galis. But taya suggested patience. 'Let's see if we, the police, can control the situation,' he advised.

But in a few days, taya had to eat his words.

The Last Warning

One evening as I was making tea in the downstairs kitchen with Sumayya chachi, Farhana came running from outside, screaming 'Baji!' in a terrified voice. She had just stepped outside to go to her tuition class. I went running towards her thinking she had been attacked. Instead, she handed me a notice. Someone had pasted it on our door.

> Consider this the last warning, from the Young Revolutionaries of 14 February to His Majesty's rented coolie soldiers.
>
> You have the blood of this country on your hands. We gave you warnings in your own languages, be they Hindi, Urdu, Arabic or Malayalam. Instead of heeding them, you continue to act without common humanity towards the innocents of this country. This proves that you are nothing but shameless slaves who do not deserve even the mud of this country.
>
> So far we have desisted from using our right to defence, hoping and expecting that you would refrain from attacking peaceful protesters, women and children.

148

But time shows that you lack both common sense and decency.

Even if we could forgive you for attacking and killing the poor people of this country, we cannot forget the circumstances that have forced us to kill the poor among you.

So please accept this advice for your own good. If you wish to save your lives, please pack your belongings and return to wherever you came from. Stop following the illegal, immoral instructions of His Majesty's government. Our people have decided to put an end to this criminal administration. Rest assured, if you continue to help him hang on to his power, you will be the first targets of our revolution.

We also ask all foreign embassies to denounce His Majesty's government for using their citizens as slave soldiers. Please take steps to recall your citizens. We will not be responsible for whatever happens to these coolie soldiers and their families if this last warning is not heeded.

Beloved people of our own country, if these mercenaries do not return to their lands, you are free to take whatever actions are necessary to protect yourself from them and to preserve your dignity. The world is a witness to your struggle for freedom. Victory will be ours.

Young Revolutionaries of 14 February

'Who pasted this on our door?' I shouted at Farhana as if she was guilty. Poor girl, what did she know. I was, in fact, more terrified than she was and was taking it out on her. By then Sippy auntie and the other women were in the kitchen and we all started panicking. Clearly, this letter had been intended for the men of our house.

We didn't let Farhana go to her tuition class. When taya came, we showed him the notice. He tried to dismiss it at first. 'Oh, this is just some boys playing a prank.'

But Sippy auntie did not let it go. 'We have three or four of our men in the police force. Don't their lives have any value?'

That evening, we gathered around the dining table and talked. We had almost decided that the women and children should go home to Pakistan and the men should stay back. If the situation improved, the women could return. Or else the men would join them. But then Farhana exploded. She had never expressed an opinion before. But that day, faced with the question of her own survival, that little girl finally spoke up.

'Why should I return to Pakistan?' she asked. 'I was born here, I grew up here, and I have every right to continue my life here. I am not going to run away, scared. This land belongs to me just as much as it belongs to the protesters.'

Her speech changed the tide of our decision-making. Every word of hers was true. This city where we had made our homes for so long – were we to pack up everything and leave like refugees, simply because of a few threats? And abandon our men to fight alone? Besides where would we find peace? What city was safe? Karachi, Lahore, Faisalabad, Hyderabad, Peshawar? Was there any street in the world where walking home safely could be guaranteed? Life was a gamble anywhere in the world. Why jump from the frying pan into the fire?

Free Countries

No one knew what was going on any more. People talked and talked, one had no idea what part of it was true, what was exaggeration, what was fiction. We believed what we wanted to believe and dismissed as falsehoods what we didn't like to hear. The protesters launched a Facebook page called '14 February Day of Rage', claiming that the government media was publishing only one side of the story. They uploaded videos of the military destroying vehicles, dragging men through the streets and kicking women.

In response, the government started a new Facebook page called 'We Love the City'. On this page, you could see videos of protesters attacking police and ordinary citizens or burning public property. Now the two sides were in a Facebook war.

Thus we started seeing what was actually happening in the City through videos on both pages. But this only increased our terror. It turned out that so much of what we had dismissed as fiction was actually true.

Slowly taya came around to establishing a checkpost in our gali. He had to admit that the police were useless. The young men of our street started the checkpost and took turns guarding it morning and night. Anyone coming and going through our gali was subject to a thorough examination. Soon they had turned our gali into a 'Free Pakistan'. They were not alone in this. All over the City, neighbourhoods were turning into countries, with Bangladeshis and Syrians and Sudanese securing their borders. Who could stop them? Only the Indians were left out. They did not organize themselves or guard their galis. Instead, they were scattered around the city, like islands. For the first time ever, I heard the Malayalam Mafia led by Viju Prasad criticize India and Indians, lamenting their own lack of community spirit.

It was the children of the City who were most affected by this atmosphere of terror. That included our own Alisha. At first we didn't take it seriously, but soon we came to understand how traumatic life had become for them.

It began when Alisha started refusing to go to school. 'The police will come and take me away from school. They will put me in an ambulance.' We tried to allay her fears, but she kept asking, 'Then why are there so many ambulances on the streets?'

'But those are for taking away people who fight in the streets! Not schoolchildren,' I told her.

'But sometimes I fight with my mama. Maybe they will catch me for that,' she replied. Then she started worrying about the checkpost. What if they didn't let her in one day?

It was no use trying to comfort her. Fear had conquered her little heart.

That night Ali posted on Twitter: 'Today's news is tomorrow's history. Let's make news!'

Emergency Care

One day Sippy auntie and I went to the market in her car to buy some necessities. It wasn't that late. Maybe eight or eight-thirty at the most. Suddenly someone came running out of a gali and fell in front of our car. Sippy auntie stepped on the brake with all her might. Luckily the tyres shrieked to a stop just before the car touched him. If we had been going at a higher speed, we would have definitely run him over. Sippy auntie got out of the car swearing at him and his ancestors, and I followed her. The man managed to get to his feet. His face and body were covered in blood. We stared at him wondering whether he had hurt himself in the fall or before that.

'Help!' he screamed and got into our car. He sat cowering in the back seat and begged us, 'Didi, please let's go away. They are still in that gali, and they have knives and sticks and axes. They will attack you too.' We got into the car quickly without thinking and drove away as fast as we could.

On the way he told us what had happened. He too had gone to the market. But a group of young men had ambushed him, hitting him with an axe. That's when I noticed the wound on his shoulder. His arm was barely hanging on to his shoulder. 'I have other wounds on my back and my legs. Please drop me off in front of a hospital,' he said to us.

But how could we simply leave him in front of a hospital in this condition? We drove to the emergency room of the medical college.

That's when we realized that as wounds go, what he had was nothing. Ambulances were screeching into the campus with people much more deeply injured. What was even more shocking was that no one was taking care of the wounded. Each new person simply sat there bleeding away. I left the man with Sippy auntie and went inside. I found a nurse at the nurse station and told her that I had a gravely wounded man with me. She looked at me scornfully. In fact, she looked at me as if I had committed some crime. 'He didn't get wounded doing anything good, did he? He was attacking our people. Let him lie there. We'll bury him when he dies,' she said.

For a moment, even my tongue went numb. I stared at her. 'Don't gape at me,' she went on. 'This hospital is not for your likes. This is for our own people.' Then she turned on her heel and went away.

I didn't know what to do. On my way back, I found a doctor. I stopped him and showed him my Orange Radio identity card, hoping that might influence him. Then I told him what I had come for. 'Come with me,' he said. 'I'll show you wards full of men and women who have been beaten up by the policemen from your country. Should I treat them or should I treat people like you who go around singing that bastard's praises? Don't think you will find any help here. If you are so worried about some pig you found on the street, why don't you take him to your hospital? We will not waste even a drop of medicine on you.' He was almost trembling with rage as he finished.

I turned around and walked away. When doctors and nurses at the medical college of a country start talking about your people and our people, there is nothing more to say.

Luckily I found an Indian nurse. When I told her my predicament, she said, 'We can't do anything without a doctor's prescription.' Then she looked around and said, 'But come with me, I'll try and give him whatever medicine I can get my hands on.'

Somehow we managed to bring the wounded man to the first aid room where she was waiting for us. When he took off his shirt, I was astounded by the extent of his wounds.' I am going to make a temporary bandage, but you should get this stitched somewhere else,' the nurse said. Just as she began working on him, the first nurse I had seen barged in. 'How dare you treat him?' she asked.

'I don't need anyone's permission to treat a wounded man. I know that much about medical ethics,' the Indian nurse retorted.

'I am going to teach you a lesson,' the first nurse said and went away.

'They are all the same. This is the arrogance we have to put up with nowadays,' the Indian nurse went on. 'I don't even care about keeping the job any more. But I can't bring myself to turn away wounded people.'

By then, the wounded man's relatives had arrived there. They thanked us for saving his life and decided to take him to another hospital.

When we got out, there seemed to be a commotion. An ambulance had arrived with several gravely wounded Bangladeshi men stuffed into its back. Their hands were tied. The hospital workers were dragging them out of the ambulance while hitting them and yelling, 'These dogs tried to attack our people.'

Whether they were attackers or rioters, at that moment they were, above all, people in need of medical care. Instead they were being beaten up in front of the hospital. Not a single policeman was to be seen anywhere nearby. Law and order had completely broken down and anyone could do anything. The City was spinning out of control.

Religious Instruction

As the problems escalated, the number of Friday visitors to Taya Ghar decreased. Perhaps they knew that their visits were pointless as taya was too busy to find jobs for them or solve their problems. Only Baluchi Barber and Karim chacha kept visiting. Chamar chacha was not to be seen in the streets. I had shoes for him to repair but I took comfort in knowing that he must be hiding at home, safe and sound. But one day when I went with Aisha auntie and Alisha to the hospital, I saw him on the veranda. There were bandages all over his face and his hand was in a cast. He came running to us. 'What happened to you?' Aisha auntie asked. 'Some young men beat me up on the street when I was sitting there sewing a sandal,'he said, and before leaving to go to the pharmacy, he asked us to convey his greetings to taya.

I couldn't understand. Why would a poor cobbler get beaten up? What could they get out of him? What do they lose from his existence in this country? Does he take away jobs from them? Is he getting rich at their expense? Those were the usual allegations against us foreigners. Brimming with resentment, I decided to ask Ali about this.

As we were leaving, we saw a huge group of doctors, nurses and paramedical staff getting ready to march to the Square of Pearls. We watched them. There were a lot of journalists reporting on their march. They were interviewing the protesters, some of whom had covered their faces.

One of the nurses made a big scene. In front of a TV reporter, she took a photo of His Majesty off the wall and tore it to pieces and stomped on it, while saying insulting things about him. A crowd formed around her and the protesters applauded her. No one discouraged her.

'I am getting a little scared, Sameera. We should avoid this camera,' Aisha auntie took my hand and dragged me away. Even as we sneaked out through another door, the nurse continued her performance.

While the number of visitors to Taya Ghar was reducing, the number of refugees was increasing. Many of our friends were fleeing neighbourhoods that were no longer safe for them. They abandoned their houses and came to Taya Ghar and taya could not refuse them. The number of beds in the bachelor rooms increased by the day.

'Where is this going to end if you let every homeless person come and live here?' Sippy auntie asked.

'They haven't come to stay forever. They just need a safe space while things are bad. How can we say no to that?' taya said.

'Then why don't you ask every Pakistani in this country to just come here right away?'

'If it is necessary, I will.'

After much argument, Sippy auntie had to give in, perhaps for the first time in her life.

One day Mustafa chacha came to our house and sat there weeping. He had a car workshop in a village in the middle of the country. 'Teach me to be a Shia. Or find someone to teach me to be a Shia,' he kept saying. The Pakistanis of the City looked on taya and Sippy auntie as encyclopaedias.

Since taya was not there at the time, Sippy auntie delegated me to handle the situation. Mustafa chacha told me that a friend of his had accidentally strayed into a Shia village recently. When the young men of the village stopped him, he said that he was a Shia. They questioned him. Name the twelve imams. Where were they born? What other names are they known by? Where are their graves? What are the places where they prayed? What's the name of the twelfth imam who fell into meditative unconsciousness? They cross-questioned him. Not only did he not know the answer to even one of the questions, he also answered the first question by reciting the nicknames of the twelve imams. These were names used by the Sunnis to taunt the Shias. The villagers beat him to pulp and abandoned him on the side of a highway. He was rescued by a patrolling police car.

Mustafa chacha lived and worked in a Shia region of the country. He could be attacked any time. Maybe when he was working, maybe when he was returning home, maybe when he was shopping, maybe when he was eating in a restaurant, maybe even when he was at home behind lock and key. There were no longer any safe places. Little wonder then that he wanted to keep a little Shia knowledge in stock. I had nothing to offer him so I roped in Khalid chacha and we gave him a crash course in Shia history and beliefs. Dear God, I hope my Shia 'beliefs' were more or less accurate. Otherwise, poor Mustafa chacha would pay dearly for it.

Believers

It was the day after the university students clashed. I was at the studio drinking coffee when I heard a commotion outside the canteen. An argument that began with soft voices had turned into a scuffle. When I ran outside, I saw Laila hitting and spitting on Yunus who was on the floor. What was going on? Meera Maskan and I held her back. She was snarling like a wild animal. But even though we stopped her, Ali and Nazar went on beating poor Yunus up.

The argument had started between Ali and Yunus. In the middle of a heated conversation about the protests, Yunus had said, 'So while you are hanging out on the street in the name of the revolution, your houses are turning into brothels.' Before anyone could stop them, there was a fist fight right there in front of the reception desk. Then Nazar had joined Ali in beating up Yunus. That was especially sad, because till then Nazar had been Yunus's best friend. Then Laila piled on. And though John Maschinas came running out of his office and yelled at them to stop, though Sheela Garments pranced around them like a cat, mewing 'Please, please', though Viju Prasad and Shahbaz and Minesh tried to separate them, the beatings went on. Long-hidden resentments had finally surfaced. Like children, they scratched and spat, bit and hit.

Finally, we had to call the security staff. By then Ali's shirt was in tatters. There were deep bite marks on Yunus's face. Hasan's eyes were swollen. The security guards asked them to leave the studio complex. For better or worse, they didn't know that Laila was also part of the fight.

Even as they left, they kept fighting with words, challenging each other. Ali cursed every caliph in the Prophet's lineage. Yunus abused all the Shia imams. They threatened to kill each other.

After that incident, Ali and Yunus never returned to the office.

Sheela Garments

The next day when I arrived at the office, Sheela Garments was running around as if his house was on fire. He was too frantic to even say what the matter was.

'I need to go out urgently right now. Just for a short while. But I'll come back soon,' he said.

'So why don't you go then instead of running around in a frenzy?'

'But I have to get permission from Imthiaz sir. He is not here yet.'

'Why don't you just go instead of waiting for Imthiaz sir? If necessary, you can always take a half-day off.'

But he didn't want to lose any vacation time. He was determined to complete this urgent task during office hours. What a miser, I thought to myself. Only after I assured him that I would tell Imthiaz sir and make sure he didn't lose his vacation time did he go. Even then, he couldn't bring himself to tell me where he was going or why. And I didn't ask either.

You are probably wondering why this poor man is called Sheela Garments. That's the nickname that the Malayalam

Mafia had given him. He is a senior clerk in our office and his real name is Philip Mathew. He would always take on any work that anyone in the office gave him and promise to finish it in two days. The next time he even remembers that piece of work is when you go back to him in two days. He would promise to attend to it right away. And then he would forget again.

At first I didn't know why Philip sir was called 'Sheela Garments'. It was Viju Prasad who had baptized him and one day he told me why. There was a tailoring shop in Viju Prasad's home town called Sheela Garments. The tailor there always promised to finish any sewing job you gave him in two days. Just like Philip sir, the tailor would even start working on your material right in front of your eyes. The moment you left the shop, he would toss the cloth under the table and get on with his life. Then when you came back in two days to get your shirt or dress, he would go, 'Ayyo, what to say, I got so busy with some urgent work. You sit right here, son. I'll take care of your work right away.' He would retrieve your cloth from under the table or wherever it was and get his scissors out and make a lot of busy cut-cut noises with them. The round chalk would come out and he would draw some lines up and down the cloth. To see him work so hard you would think the shirt would be done in ten minutes. 'Okay, why don't you go for a walk in the town? By the time you come back, I'll keep this all ironed and pretty.' Again the promise. The moment you left the shop, your cloth would go back under the table.

Philip sir was cast in the same mould. As soon as he saw you, he would launch into the story of how busy he had got since he promised to do the job you gave him. He would apologize a hundred times for forgetting. He would find all your files and put them right on top of his desk. He would open the programme and the folders he needed on his computer and would even start entering the data. Thank God, you think. As you walked back to your desk relieved that the job was going to get done right away, Philip sir would turn into Sheela Garments.

Viju Prasad had told this story to everyone in the office, including Maschinas sir. And everyone agreed that Philip sir deserved this name. So Sheela Garments was the most famous nickname in our office, the first nickname that newcomers learned.

Imthiaz sir did not arrive that day even by noon. But Sheela Garments returned in a couple of hours. He looked as if he had accomplished something huge, and thanked me for encouraging him to leave.

'So what was your urgent business?' I could not control my curiosity any more.

'Yesterday there was a rumour,' Sheela Garments pulled his chair towards mine and whispered, 'that they were going to shut down all the banks and money exchanges. People were saying it would become impossible to send money anywhere, that the currency would become seriously devalued. I was just praying that nothing like that would happen till I got to the bank this morning. Luckily the banks were still open. But can you imagine how crowded it was at the bank? Everyone was sending all their money home. Now I have done that too. I cannot even buy a safety pin now. Let them shut the banks or destroy them or whatever.'

Then Sheela Garments shared his news with everyone in the office. As soon as they heard this, the Malayalam Mafia, who were bigger cowards than Sheela Garments, cursed him for not saying anything earlier, and immediately hurried off to the money exchanges. Why blame them? We all remember how Iraqi money and Kuwaiti money turned into origami paper the day after the war began.

By then the rumour had become hot news in the City. Long lines appeared in front of banks and money exchanges and ATMs. Many poor labourers from Nepal and Bangladesh who had no way of transferring money ran to the gold exchanges and bought gold biscuits with all their money. All these fears became real the next day when the banks shut down temporarily. Money exchange systems froze. The withdrawal limit at ATMs was cut by two-thirds. And Viju Prasad, who had been the only one in the Malayalam Mafia to mock Sheela Garments and make light of his fears, hit his head with his hands and wept.

Freedom of News

Around us, the news was always at boiling temperature. BBC and other foreign media were broadcasting every bit of breaking news. But at our radio station, the music concerts continued. When someone is getting skewered above a hot fire, can you amuse them by tickling their armpits? Sumayya, our regular newscaster, was away on vacation and I was subbing for her, otherwise I might not have noticed all this.

Hasan would translate news from the different corners

of the City. Imthiaz sir and I would run to Rajeevan sir's office with it. We wanted to run it as breaking news or spot news. But Rajeevan sir would completely reject our ideas. There is no need to report all this, he would say. We were also instructed to show him every news report before it was aired. And unusually, he would wait in the studio till we did so.

Even as the City lived in fear, our channels alone continued the good life relentlessly with songs, raffles, and funny quizzes. We were told to air only fast songs. Even I felt annoyed and sad after a while. I decided that whether they liked it or not, the next bulletin would contain some real news. I prepared my news report and went to our chairman. He read it and gaped as if to ask what the hell I had written.

'Sir, when there are so many problems in the City, what's the point of us playing ostrich and burying our heads in the sand. Haven't you seen all the text messages cursing us? I can't keep pretending to be blind. If you cut even one sentence out of this bulletin, I will not read the news any more.'

He stared at me for a minute. Perhaps he hadn't expected such a reaction.

'You are right, Sameera. I, too, would like to talk about the City's problems in every bulletin of ours. It is our duty to give our listeners advice and warnings. But do you know, we have been prohibited from up above from mentioning any real news. We are obliged to follow that prohibition. You have been here for a while. Have you ever seen me meddling with the news reports? This is not just about my survival, it's for the sake of all of you. If there is even a small lapse, that's the end of our radio station. I worked hard to create this station. Fifteen years of my life went into building it from scratch. I cannot let one moment of recklessness destroy that. If that makes me selfish, go ahead, call me selfish. That's why I sit here day and night. I am constantly in touch with the ministry and the government. I keep telling them the people are living in fear and we need to give them at least some real information. But always the answer is 'wait'. If you still don't understand my position, go ahead and read this bulletin.'

He returned the news report without cutting a single line.

I went and sat at my table, with my head bowed. For a moment I felt scornful towards myself, my life. If I could have spat in my own face, I would have. Then I tore up the report and went to the editorial table to prepare a new draft.

That night, I wrote on Twitter: 'When there is no freedom of press, rumour becomes news.'

Partition

In those days of protest, if there was a radio station that took the City's problems seriously and tried to broadcast real news, it was Hit Arabia. They ignored the prohibitions and conducted live debate programmes and reported attacks. They interviewed both protesters and those who were against the protests, without any bias. Women from all over the country called Hit Arabia to tell them about how they were suffering and how their loved ones were attacked. Women who had lost their fathers and husbands and brothers in earlier conflicts wept about their fears for their children. They requested their sons and daughters to return from the protests. They could not bear to think of losing their children in yet another round of persecution.

Salman from String Walkers often did live shows at Hit Arabia during those days. One day I listened to him for a bit. He knew exactly how to console his audience. He poured comfort and energy into their ears, cautioning, encouraging, reassuring, and empathizing with those mothers.

This was the same Salman who had walked out of String Walkers after quarrelling with Ali. In the beginning, many, like Salman, were pro-protests. I had often heard him agreeing with Ali. His attitude was that His Majesty had had his turn, now it was time for a new era. He was not alone. After all, the entire world had moved towards democracy. Why shouldn't we enjoy those freedoms, for better or worse, people asked.

There were no religious symbols in those protests. There were no photos of imams or sheikhs and no slogans in their support. The only flags were the national flag and the white flag of peace. Some maulvis would come to the Square to give speeches. But so did politicians, human rights workers, communists and social justice activists. They all had the freedom to give speeches and many different organizations had put up their tents there. No single leader could claim to represent all the protesters.

But the anti-government protest quickly turned into a sectarian protest. Or perhaps it was portrayed like that and pushed in that direction. What was a protest by the people against the injustices of His Majesty turned into a protest by

Shias against Sunnis. Soon there was a feeling that Sunnis would have to fight for their lives, that if the majority came to power, the Sunni minority would be persecuted. As that fear grew, the Sunnis decided to betray the protests and help defeat it. And Salman was one of them.

The Master and the Management

I could sense that taya was worrying over whether his worst fears would come to pass. Till then he had scorned the protesters and thought of them as wastrels with unwarranted demands. But now his scorn disappeared. He could feel them growing stronger in the streets while the reins held by the police got looser and looser.

He was always angry in those days. His Majesty and the government had not authorized the police to take strong action against the protesters. Apparently, His Majesty had said, 'They are my children and they have every right to protest in my streets.' But taya kept fuming about the secret forces that were plotting the fall of the government.

'Twenty-four hours, that's all we need. Just twenty-four hours. Leave the streets to us. I will show you what we can do. But His Majesty's advisers are those retired senile old men from Scotland Yard. What do they know of this country?' he kept muttering.

One day he brought home all our passports from the office. Since all leave had been cancelled, the passports would never have been handed over. But using his influence, taya had got hold of them. He advised the uncles who were not working in the police department to get their passports back as well from their employers and prepare to leave the country in case of an emergency.

As Pakistanis continued to be attacked in our streets, we had few options. We knew that the moment the government fell, we would be at the mercy of the protesters. Especially those who worked in the police force. Everyone knew that taya was a senior police officer. The protesters would use Taya Ghar for target practice. After all, it was the stronghold of the mercenaries! The Kadhim al-Jubouris of the City were waiting to tear it down.

We started preparing to leave that very night. The suitcases that were stored under the beds and on top of cupboards came out for dusting and packing. They were covered with luggage tags and security check stickers from many previous journeys. But they were all symbols of happy holidays, eagerly awaited vacations. This would be a different kind of journey. An abandonment. An exile. This time, the suitcases were only for the most important possessions, the ones that could not be left behind. I did not have to spend too much time choosing. The guitar from baba, my laptop, a few clothes – that was all. But imagine having to fill ten or twenty years' worth of life into one suitcase. All those things that you scrimped and saved for over the years. Sippy auntie and Aisha auntie were in that position. Just the packing made them cry. Sippy auntie had always imagined living out the rest of her life in this house, in this City. 'Why should we have to go? And where? Who are we so scared of? This is our country too. Don't we have any rights here? I did not know your taya was such a coward,' she kept mumbling as if in a delirium.

Aisha auntie had enough books to fill three airplanes. To pick two or three books out of her entire collection and discard the rest was akin to cutting off a piece of her heart. Somehow, in between weeping, she managed to condense her belongings to thirty kilos.

It was not just Taya Ghar. Households around the City were weighing and measuring, choosing and packing. Ma called every day from the village, asking baba and me to return as soon as possible. She couldn't understand why we couldn't just get on the next plane and come home to her. Baba was at work twenty-four hours. Why don't you just quit, ma asked. She did not have the worldly experience to understand why that was impossible.

Only Khalid chacha did not get ready to go home. He decided that he would stay on in the City, for better or worse, life or death. That was not because of any great fondness for the City.

Khalid chacha has a special relationship with his boss. He worked in a small air-conditioning workshop. He often got paid late or not at all. I asked him once why he worked for so little. With his experience, he could have easily got a cushier job. Chacha told me the story of how he met his boss. When chacha was walking down a gali one night, he saw a drunk man in front of a restaurant trying unsuccessfully to insert the key in the door of his car. He stopped chacha and asked him to help. Chacha was happy to open his car for him. Then the man asked if he knew how to drive. Chacha knew how to drive but didn't have a licence. Never mind that, just get this car out of the parking lot, the man requested. Chacha did that too. Then the man said that he was in no condition to drive and would probably not get home safe if he did drive. He asked chacha to drive him home. Chacha reminded him that he didn't have a licence. 'Don't worry, if anything happens I'll take care of it,' the car owner said. Chacha took him home. On the way, asked chacha where he worked. Chacha replied that he was looking for a job. The man told him to start the next day as his driver. Since that day, chacha has been his trusted assistant, driver, accountant, and overseer.

Taya and others kept advising chacha that he should look out for himself and try to make some money during his working life in the City. But chacha could never bring himself to leave his boss. Until recently, I thought he was bluffing. But it was in those troubled days that I understood the depth of their affection for each other. Everyday chacha's boss called us to find out if we were okay. One day when the roads were impassable and the shops were shut down, he somehow came to Taya Ghar bringing with him rice, wheat, sugar, tea, milk powder and water. He gave chacha some money in case of an emergency.

None of us had a good answer when chacha asked us how he could leave such a good man. Javed, that's when I realized what an old-fashioned master–servant relationship was really about. Yes, those old-time masters were mere shopkeepers. But they were also men of flesh and blood. They had consciences. On the other hand, the management at the studio told us that regardless of the problems in the City, we were expected to turn up for work every day on time. There would be no compromises. Nobody in the management had the courage to go against the law. That is the difference between corporate managements with their bureaucratic legalisms and an old-fashioned master with a heart. Unlike our management, he had the good sense to understand the circumstances we were all living in.

Riots

One day when I was hosting a live show, Fathima madam came running into the switch room in panic. Since we were playing a song just then, I stepped out to find out what was happening.

'There is a crowd outside the main gate of our studio. They are stopping passers-by and beating up some people,' she said. 'We should all leave the studio immediately. They are checking the IDs before hitting people, so be careful.'

It was one of those rare days when Rajeevan sir and Imthiaz sir and other senior managers were not at work. There were only a few junior staff, including Shahbaz and me at the Hindi station, Viju Prasad and Sharon at the Malayalam station, Kapil bhai at the switchboard, and Sasikala in the office. We didn't know what to do. All the others, it seemed, had abandoned us for their own safety. I was furious. I just wanted to get home somehow.

The Malayalam Mafia called Rajeevan sir immediately. He told us not to stay back for any of the live shows. Just put some songs on and go home right away. Then we called our new driver. But there was too much traffic on the streets for him to reach soon.

By then I was really worried. The men would somehow get home safely. But what would happen to me? If someone on the road inspected my ID and found that I was a Pakistani . . . Both Sippy auntie and Aisha auntie had told me this morning not to go. If only I had listened to them. I called baba but his phone was switched off. For the last few days, he had not even come home.

When I called Taya Ghar, Khalid chacha offered to come and get me, but I wouldn't let him. The rioters were especially targeting Pakistanis nowadays. They would never let chacha get past them. I told him I would somehow manage on my own.

Viju Prasad understood my anxiety. He approached me. 'Please don't worry, Sameera. No one will hurt you. We won't go home till we take you home.' I was surprised to hear this from the person who had always picked on me.

We all left together right away. The main gate of the station was locked but through its bars we could see some people waiting outside. The watchman told us to use the back gate. We got out and waited for a taxi. There were very few vehicles on the road and the one or two taxis that came by did not even stop for us. Viju called a taxi driver he knew. He asked for three times the normal fare but we didn't have any other option, so we agreed. He came in fifteen minutes and the six of us, including Sasikala, the Malayalam Mafia and I squeezed in.

We only realized the gravity of the situation after the car started moving. The streets were littered with tyres, stones and sticks. In the first five minutes, we saw more than fifteen smashed cars. Our driver told us that there had been a huge clash at the university again. Hundreds of students were in the hospital and many vehicles had been destroyed. He himself had escaped narrowly.

As we reached the next roundabout, we saw a crowd of about fifty people, armed with guns and sticks. They stopped our vehicle and asked the driver to lower the windows. I bowed my head behind Viju and tried to disappear. For the first time in my life, I was afraid to reveal that I was Pakistani. One of the men checked the driver's ID and that of Kapil bhai who was sitting in the passenger seat. I was trembling. I could be captured any moment.

But luck was with me that day. After just glancing at the back seat, he gestured that we could go. I think they only saw Sasikala and the other men.

As the light turned green and we started moving forward, a car sped by us from the opposite direction, without waiting for their turn. Somebody was making a run for their life. They might have easily hit us. By the time we reached Taya Ghar, we had passed many such cars.

That day, the Malayalam Mafia, who had always argued that they should get home first, took me all the way home. Even Sasikala, who could have got off on the way, insisted on accompanying me to my door.

In the face of adversity, there is no you and me. National borders disappear. Office resentments melt. There is just 'we' and 'us'. I was moved to tears by their tenderness for me that day.

Facebook

Taya Ghar was waiting for me. As soon as I got home, Sippy auntie began scolding me for not listening to her in the morning. What could I say to her when I knew that her anger was actually her fear for my life? A sudden sadness overwhelmed me. All that tension that I had somehow bottled up that day suddenly exploded into tears. Aisha auntie and Farhana comforted me. They made me coffee and served me some food. Slowly, I calmed down.

Later, I switched on the TV to find out what was going on. I was shocked to see what was playing on the national TV channel – His Majesty, who was visiting a neighbouring country, was holding a sword and dancing with some traditional dancers. His country was rapidly descending into riots, but he was dancing. It was as if he was mocking his own people, their longing for freedom, their anxiety about their lives. I threw the remote on the floor and turned to my laptop. Viju Prasad had posted a status on Facebook and there was a stream of comments. The subject, of course, was the situation in the City. I read through them without commenting. Though some of the comments were in their language, I could still understand the emotions of the commenters.

Viju Prasad: The protesters have fully taken over the streets. Very frightening. I am checking in on Google Real Time. A power cut might be possible. Be prepared.

Minesh Menon: Did you see what's on TV? Our honourable Majesty is dancing and enjoying himself.

Shahbaz: I saw that. There have always been emperors who played the fiddle while their countries burned. Time to figure out how to protect ourselves.

Viju Prasad: I just returned from our studio. Protesters with guns and sticks are everywhere and they are examining everyone's IDs. We escaped somehow. Where are the police?

Sharon: Nattilekku poyalo ennalochikkunnu. But no ticket. Kittiyal najangl pokum. Whr is police? . . . Whr is national bird?!!

Dilbasuran: Just heard that a Pakistani has been stabbed. According to Twitter, there will be a hartal tomorrow.

Viju Prasad: Lots of fake news on Twitter. Very biased messages. We should not think of Twitter as a reliable source.

Sharon: Why are they attacking the greenies and Bangladeshis?

Minesh Menon: Coz they are Sunnis. And protesters are angry at those who participated in the rally against them.

Anamika: Pls all sit at home only. Don't go outside, any news pls update. I am here only.

Kunjan Praveen: That's not the only reason they are targeting Bangladeshis and Pakistanis. We Malayalis will hide in our holes the moment we hear of a problem. We know how to look out for our own safety.

Jayan: Hot news . . . hot news . . . emergency to be declared in the country today or tomorrow.

Anamika: Emergency . . .? Then enthokkeya athinte paridhiyil varunnathu? Jolikku povunnathu okke enthavun avastha? If somebody knows, paranju tharuka.

Sharon: Will have to check the constitution, Anamika.

Ashwathi Pillai: If possible, send your families home.

Kunjan Praveen: Yeah right, what about the children's schools and exams?

Rickson Kuriakose: Kunja, isn't their health and life more important than some examinations? Besides, are the schools still functioning where you are?

Dilbasuran: I hear that the Gulf countries are going to send their armies. His Majesty has invited the Peninsula Shield Force to support the government following anti-government demonstrations in the capital.

Viju Prasad: Peninsula Shield Force (https://en.wikipedia.org/wiki/Peninsula_Shield_Force) has about 7000 soldiers. There are also unconfirmed reports that the British Foreign Office has instructed all its citizens, including journalists, to leave the country.

Jayan: I heard that they have opened an emergency room at the hospital in Airport City. They are also recruiting immediately. If there are any unemployed nurses, this is a good opportunity.

Anil Vasudev: Apparently that hospital was opened because the medical college is under the control of the protesters and they won't let foreigners and others get treatment there.

Ranji: I can hear ambulances.

Anamika: Evide anu ambulance?

Anil Vasudev: Shiite groups say that arrival of foreign troops in country is a declaration of war.

Viju Prasad: Tens of thousands are ready to be martyrs and have already dressed up for death.

Ranji: Forty-five ambulances just arrived at the medical college.

Minesh Menon: A native of the City just tweeted this: 'No matter what happens, just remember that we're all brothers and sisters. We studied, played, ate, laughed and cried together.'

Smitha Gopinath: Like this 10,000 times.

Dilbasuran: Curfew will probably be declared tonight or tomorrow. Fill your vehicles with petrol and stock up on groceries, especially canned foods. Don't forget candles, drinking water. If possible get your passports from your employers. If the situation worsens, our sponsors will not think twice about leaving the country themselves.

Viju Prasad: For everyone's attention. Just got this message. The protesters have been warned to vacate the Square. If they don't, there will be military action. Emergency has been declared and the army has been posted in various parts of the city. Curfews have been announced and tomorrow will be a public holiday.

Ashwathi Pillai: My hubby just went to the store to buy some essential groceries. He had to go to five or six stores. They were all crowded. People are carrying away their groceries in trolleys. Once the stocks are finished, there won't be any supplies. So go and stock up. Anything could happen.

Anamika: national bird starts flying again ... which area having problems ...?

Kunjan Praveen: Above my house, every two minutes there are national birds flying in the same direction, without their lights on. The atmosphere feels very tense. People are standing on their rooftops watching. I didn't spend much time up there because of the cold, but I can still see them through the windows.

Mullookkaran: Shoot one down, Kunja. That will show them.

Kunjan Praveen: I did pick up a stone, boss. Then thought, never mind.

Ashwathi Pillai: I am praying that everyone is safe.

Minesh Menon: What is the situation in the Square of Pearls? Are the protesters still there, or have they vacated?

Ranjith: Is the embassy doing anything to help people?

Kunjan Praveen: Yeah, right. They have instructed everyone to stay indoors. Big deal. Oh, also this. I got a form from them asking for all my information. Except of course the passport number. What are they going to do without that number? What's the point of filling up the form?

Jayesh Alukka: Kunja, what form do we have to fill? Is there any use? Is it available online?

Minesh Menon: I have registered with them anyway. Maybe they will organize a ship for repatriating us!!

Kunjan Praveen: Boss, I am doubtful. I am guessing the emergency scenario in this country will be different from an Emergency in India. But it's been a while since they declared it and they haven't given any information on what we can do and what we can't. Why doesn't our embassy give us more info on their website? Shouldn't they be rising to the occasion? If anyone from the embassy is reading this, please tell us how to prepare ourselves. We don't need an embassy to tell us to sit home and twiddle our thumbs!

Ranji Ranji: Supposedly, the foreign ministry is observing the situation very carefully. Didn't you hear the deputy foreign minister saying yesterday that expats should stay calm? If there is a sudden exodus, the Indian embassy will be in as much hassle as any other embassy. The Australian, British and French embassies have given their people an 'emergency baggage' message – that means you should pack an emergency bag with your travel documents, some clothes and first aid. Let's also do the same. Our embassy probably won't care if we rot to death here. They'll be like, what's the big deal, it's not like we really need you back home.

Minesh Menon: I think it is good that they finally declared an Emergency, if indeed they did so. At least someone is in charge of law and order now.

VM: Take care. Hope your loved ones are all safe. Stay away from anything unnecessary. Godspeed and goodnight.

Ashwathi Pillai: Take care. And update your statuses when you can. That itself is a big help.

Jayan: Does everyone have their passports? If you don't feel comfortable, don't go to office tomorrow. I pray for everyone's safety. Good night.

Anamika: Kidannal urakkam varilla . . . Urangiyal kanunnathu pedi swapnangalum . . .!! Ennalum ellavarkum shubha rathri!

Minesh Menon: Good night all . . . TC

Curfew

Announcement from the General Command of the National Defence Force

16 March: A curfew has been imposed starting tomorrow and until further notice between 4 p.m. and 4 a.m. in the City. The residents should coordinate with the checkpoints to facilitate their movement officially. Gatherings, rallies, demonstrations and sit-ins are not allowed anywhere in the Kingdom until the situation is back to normal.

All citizens and residents must cooperate fully with the checkpoints for their safety. Anyone who violates these measures will face appropriate legal action.

Peace and God's mercy and blessings be upon you.

Charuhassan: For everyone's attention: Here are some steps you can take in case the situation deteriorates further. You might not be able to take care of this stuff later. Some of this might not be relevant to you. Just think of these as tips that have worked well in similar situations.

1. Love your neighbour as you love yourself.
2. Do not count on the availability of the Internet.
3. Create some community networks on the basis of your neighbourhood, mobile phone and landline. Each network should have twenty to fifty members or families, depending on your circumstances and convenience. Set aside your religious, caste, political and regional affiliations and cooperate with each other. Every network should have a responsible and willing team leader.

4. Avoid creating and spreading rumours. Any news that arrives by hearsay should be confirmed by the team leaders before it is disseminated to the networks. And indicate the source of the news. Do not add any 'masala' to the news.

5. If you have an amateur radio set, keep it as ready as legally possible, and if necessary beyond those limits. Please check your connection to radio networks in India via EchoLink. Get hold of car batteries and good quality yagi antennae.

6. Avoid conversations and debates in public places such as restaurants and offices.

7. Remember that there is no privacy on the Internet. It is a public place that anyone can access. Connecting to the Internet is a luxury that can be taken away any time.

8. Those with cars should find three or four people who do not have any transport and be ready to carpool with them if necessary. Keep your cars ready to go.

9. Be willing to share your food, medicines, and other essentials.

10. Print out the addresses (local and Indian), email addresses and phone numbers of those in your network. Keep your copy on you at all times.

11. Ask your families at home to create phone networks between families of various expats so that news from here can reach more people at home easily.

12. Try to include doctors, nurses and travel agents in every network.

13. Decide on a gathering place (meeting point/collection

point/shelter) for your network in case of some emergency or evacuation.

14. Each person should secure a small multiband radio (with AM/FM/SW) and good batteries. Identify other SW stations so that you can tune in easily.

15. Ration your own use of consumer goods. Use only as much food, drinking water and gas as you need.

Minesh Menon: After reading Charu's awesome tips above, I thought I would add this – a list of dos and don'ts.

1. Keep your identity card with you at all times when you are outside your residence.

2. Ensure that there is no luggage in your car or trunk.

3. You might find yourself questioned point-blank, with a gun aimed at you. Do not panic. Your interrogators might not know English. Try to speak to them in Arabic.

4. Be specific in your answers when they ask where you are going and where you are coming from. Don't beat around the bush.

5. Do not give rides to anyone without an identity card.

6. Keep your phone and laptop fully charged at all times. When a neighbourhood is targeted for military action, the power will be cut.

7. You can leave the house if you feel brave enough, but know that you might be killed anywhere.

Ragesh Kurman: Charuvinte valuable comments inodoppam oru orukkam koode cheythu vakkam. In case of emergency: Road map till your border with 2–3 different and safe routes marked

Toolkit with all necessary tools
If possible, one additional spare tyre
Foot-operated air pump
Spare petrol can and water can
Shovel
Towing rope
Spare batteries, wires and bulbs
First aid box
Precautionary measures: Do not give away your CVs or personal information even if you receive emails or calls. Do not open the door for anyone who says they are from electricity or telephones. Be back in your homes and be aware and alert!

Oh, I forgot to add this very important point: Say No to those pimps! Don't ever even switch on those channels! Also ask your families abroad to turn them off.

I have seen them telling bloody utter lies about the very events taking place right in front of my eyes. Perhaps only the following channels are reliable:
1. BBC World
2. Euronews
3. DW
Never trust CNN!!

Many Truths

That night as I lay down to sleep, I asked myself, 'Whose side are you on? With Ali and the protesters or with baba and taya and the police?' I knew that the protesters were attacking foreigners like us, asking us to leave and harming innocents. They had censored all criticism of their activities and denied medical assistance to those who were not with them. Baba and the rest were trying to bring back law and order to the City. While they were arresting and beating up those who challenged His Majesty, they were not attacking innocents. Besides they were merely coolies from another country. Servants who had to carry out the orders of their masters. When the master said 'Hit', they hit. When the master said 'Shoot', they shot. Beyond that, they didn't have a part in all this. Even taya who huffed and puffed a lot as a senior officer did not have the power to take a single decision on his own. So who was right? Whose side should win?

If baba and the rest won, Ali and his comrades would be crushed under their heels. This country's longing for freedom would be buried, perhaps forever. The dreams they had dreamed in these last few days! Mansions to be destroyed. Masters to be hung from a noose. New laws to be executed. The people to be exiled. Aid for the poor. Jobs for those who needed them. These were the dreams of a people who had been suffering for a long time.

Having weighed both sides, I should be on His Majesty's side. The survival of his administration was the key to my livelihood and that of so many other foreign workers like me. The day the administration fell, we would be kicked out of this country. I would lose everything, my job at the studio, my friendships there, the joyful evenings at String Walkers, taya's and baba's jobs, the happiness at Taya Ghar. So many many people would lose their livelihoods. Aisha auntie and

Farhana and I would be scattered in many directions. For my own sake, it was best for the revolution to fail.

But even after thinking it all through, my heart secretly hoped that the revolutionaries would win. I don't know why. That's just the way I am. I am always on the underdog's side. Even though I want Pakistan to win in cricket matches against our arch enemy India, when I see the Indian team lose, I feel bad. Even when I join my friends and family in cheering and praying for our team, a part of me wants India to win. This was also like that. At the dining table in Taya Ghar and in the kitchen and in Cattle Class conversations and during our arguments in the studio canteen, I supported His Majesty and laughed at the protesters. But deep inside, I wanted them to win. Even more than I wanted my own survival, my own success, my own happiness, I wanted Ali to survive, Ali to succeed, Ali to be happy. Even when everyone else dismissed him, I could see that there was some truth in what he fought for. I still don't know why. And so that night as well, I prayed for him.

But my prayers went unanswered. The next day, the Peninsula Army crossed the borders and arrived in the country.

Part 5

Bolo Takbir

Death Bells

I was sound asleep when I suddenly heard loud crying, like a tidal wave of sorrow. For a while I thought I was still dreaming, that the cries were my own. I lay there with my eyes closed. By then that one sound had scattered into thousands of cries. That's when I realized that I was awake, and the cries were coming from the street beyond my balcony.

I checked the time on my mobile. Dawn was still a few hours away. The room was pitch dark. Usually, a little light from the street lamps outside would filter in even after I switched off the lights in the room. But today that was missing. I got up and switched on the lights. They did not work. That's when I realized that the City had lost power.

This is not a city where power cuts happen. In my three years here, I have never experienced a single power cut. I tried to call Aisha auntie on the phone, but the phone was not working either. The signal bars on my phone were weak. Fear started gnawing at me. Quickly I got back into bed and got under the blankets.

Baba had told me that I should not, under any

circumstances, step out on the balcony any more. It had been three days since he had come home from work. Taya told me that all the policemen were working continuously, day and night. The City had become their battlefield. I prayed for baba and stayed in bed, remembering what he and taya had told me about staying inside the room. But the cries outside were now accompanied by gunshots from further away. I could not stay in bed any longer. Like a horse straining against its bridle, my curiosity would not stay down. Still, too scared to step out on the balcony, I peeked through the curtains.

First I saw a flight of terrified doves flying out of formation in the night sky. A few minutes later, a huge crowd came running down the street, yelling and screaming. I realized that the Square of Pearls had been attacked. I could see fire and smoke in the distance. Tents were burning. Five helicopters were hovering over the Square in a half-circle and supervising the attack. People, vehicles and ambulances kept flowing through the streets. I hadn't even known that so many people were camping in the Square. I saw pick-up trucks filled with chairs, tents, kitchen vessels, televisions, flags, rugs and whatever else could be quickly removed from the camps. Ambulances tried unsuccessfully to honk their way through the crowds that were running to save their lives. Only the sound of the ambulances travelled up the street. Trucks with wounded bodies in the back tried to move through the crowds. But there was too much panic and chaos for them to make much headway. The protesters had finally broken down – they were now running away from the final fate that awaited them.

Suddenly, my doorbell rang. I started. What to do? I ran to my bed. But when the bell sounded again, I went and looked through the peephole. My two chachis were waiting outside. Relieved and grateful for the company, I opened the door. They were wondering about the sounds outside. The men had gone to the terrace to check. 'What about taya? Won't we get into trouble with him if we go to the balcony?' I asked. But taya had been called away last night on an emergency and hadn't returned yet, my chachis told me.

I wanted to go out on the balcony with them, now that there were three of us. But my chachis didn't let me do that. We sat on the floor and peeked through the curtains. The streets were still full of people and vehicles. Even then, some of those running were shouting slogans. But their voices had gone weak and the slogans sounded faint. The only thing we could hear even a bit was calls of 'Allahu Akbar'.

The crowds kept passing by for a while. Then it was just vehicles. After that, a terrible emptiness fell on the streets. Four or five lost sandals and shoes, one or two bottles of milk – which, I learnt later, is used to counter the tear gas – and a few onions were scattered here and there. We waited, expecting more people. Suddenly there was a gunshot. I saw a bullet ricochet off the divider on the road. It was barely twenty feet away from us. We looked at each other fearfully. Even then, I felt an enormous curiosity to step out on the balcony and find out what was happening there, beyond our tiny plane of vision. But my chachis refused to let me go.

For about three minutes after, the streets brooded in silence. Then, through our tiny slit in the curtain, we saw a military vehicle, moving very slowly. Two vehicles with cannons followed it and behind them were two covered vehicles with four soldiers on each. Rows of hundreds of soldiers walked behind the vehicles. They raised their guns and chanted zealously, 'Bolo Takbir . . . Allahu Akbar.'

I couldn't help smiling at the irony. Both the hunter and the prey were yelling the same slogan. The soldiers reprimanded people who had gathered to watch from their windows, balconies and rooftops. One half-naked Indian man, belly hanging out, was standing on his balcony, not simply watching, but videotaping the march. He ignored the soldiers when they asked him to stop. Suddenly there was a gunshot. Even as we watched, we saw him fall from his balcony. A scream started rising from my chachi's throat. I covered her mouth. A few people came running out of the wounded man's flat. But the soldiers ordered them back. They had no choice but to obey. The soldiers threw the man's body in the back of an army truck as if he were an old sack and went on.

Thus began the ruthless strangling of a people. It was the end of all resistance. But even then I didn't know that there were new nightmares waiting for me.

Stains in the Snow

Over the next one hour, the City quietened down. The crying and the gunshots stopped. Power was restored. Mobile signals returned. But fear lay, like a blanket of snow, on the streets.

I called the studio and got Shahbaz. Of the Orange staff, only Imthiaz sir and he had arrived in office so far and in Tunes Malayalam, Sharon, Minesh and Sheetal.

'Never mind the live music shows, we can keep throwing songs on. But news is going to be tough. Imthiaz sir will have to write all the bulletins. And there is no one at the switchboards.'

'Should I come amidst all this trouble?' I asked.

'We have orders from above that all programmes should continue as normal.' I could sense from his voice that he wanted me to come in to work.

'What are the roads like? Can I get to work?'

'The army is all over the roads and they will check all the vehicles. Since our vehicle has a station sticker, they will let you pass.'

'Okay, send the car in about half an hour.' I ran to the bathroom to get ready.

When I came downstairs, all the men and women of Taya Ghar were in a celebratory mood. It was not just that the Square of Pearls had been vacated and the protests were over. It was a relief that their jobs were safe and they did not have to leave the country. It was also arrogance that their authority was now restored. It was also a release of all the pent-up tensions of the last several days. Bhupo was distributing laddoos.

Sippy auntie almost bit my head off when I said I was off to the studio. 'For God's sake, if you are going to lose the job because you didn't turn up today, that is perfectly fine. We can't let you go on a day like this when there are soldiers trolling the streets.'

But I was determined to go. It was not that I was dying to present a radio show. But at the studio, I would hear real news from around the City. Even though we couldn't broadcast it, we would hear it all. It was always exciting to go through all that classified info. Then there was the canteen. An hour in the canteen and I would catch up on everything that had happened in the City. If I wanted to know what the situation was really like, in all its detail, I had to go there.

'Shahbaz told me the streets were peaceful. Actually, it will be safer now that the military has taken over. And if there's any trouble, I'll return immediately,' I argued.

'Never mind me then. You have a baba, you have a taya. If they let you go, then fine.' Sippy auntie washed her hands off the matter. 'And keep in mind what happened the last time. It is easy to go; the hard part is coming back.'

I knew that I would not get hold of baba. His phone had been switched off for the last three days. I called taya but didn't get through to him either. By then the driver had given me a missed call.

Aisha auntie, Khalid chacha and Anwar mamu had joined the chorus and discouraged me from going. I would happily disobey anyone, but I could not disobey Aisha auntie and Khalid chacha. So I called the driver and half-heartedly told him that I was not coming. 'Then why'd you make me come here in such a hurry? You should have decided earlier,' he said angrily.

I went up to my room, annoyed with myself and the family, and even more than that, sad. Aisha auntie followed me and knocked on my door several times but I didn't open the door. I felt ashamed of myself for sitting in my room

194

nursing my defeat. Who was I scared of? The protesters who had run scared for their lives? Or the army and police in the streets gloating over their victory? Never mind, I told myself, it's just one day. And maybe I'll make it there for the afternoon shift. But inside I was fuming. I stepped out on to the balcony. The national bird was circling the skies. I had to smile at the humour behind this nickname.

Then I saw two people walking, supporting a young man between them. He had been shot in his leg. They were trying not to be seen, walking right next to the walls. But the national bird must have spotted them with its hawk eyes. Suddenly, about twenty military vehicles came speeding out of nowhere and screeched to a stop right beneath our flat. Soldiers leaped out of those vehicles and ran into the galis. The men leaped over the wall of the park and disappeared behind the bushes. They were trying to run while holding the wounded man.

The soldiers kept firing here and there as they pursued the men. The police vehicles started moving helter-skelter up the galis, driving on the footpaths on either side and scraping parked vehicles. When the men were almost caught, a few women came running on to the street. They dragged the huge trash cans at the corners to the middle of the street. Trash spilled out. The police vehicles had to stop.

The women held hands and spread out to prevent the soldiers from running. One soldier came forward to beat them. Another aimed his gun at them. But they stood their ground. They cursed the soldiers and told them to go back. There was a girl among them, barely a teenager. She tried to grab a gun from one of the soldiers. They started wrestling. I could not believe how she held her own against that strong soldier. At one point it almost looked like she would get the gun out of his hands. But suddenly another soldier leaped into the fray and hit her below her knees with his gun. She spun around twice and fell down. The soldiers circled around her and started kicking her. They pushed away the other women who came to rescue her. Another police vehicle arrived. They flung her into the back of that vehicle. The vehicle started speeding forward throwing back the other women who tried to get on. Before the vehicle had reached the highway, I saw her tunic flying out of the window.

The Colour of Fear

I could not get that image out of my head, however hard I tried. I switched on the TV. But my eyes were barely registering its pictures. I switched on the radio. The songs did not touch me at all. I picked up a magazine. But the fashion and the gossip seemed to belong to another world. Nothing but numbness. My baba and taya and chachas and mamus were policemen and soldiers. Is this how they, too, behaved with young women? At home, they could not have been more loving. I can't remember them hurting us, with even a word or a glance. But perhaps the soldiers who had just taken away the young woman were also loving fathers and uncles and brothers at home? How did they turn into animals in heat on the street? Were all men angels at home and beasts outside it?

I had always respected and taken pride in my soldier dada

and my policemen chachas and baba. I worshipped them as warriors who fought bravely against enemies. Now I knew them to be hunters who preyed on unarmed women. Wait till baba came home. I would ask him if this was how he behaved with women. If so, we don't need this salary any more. I would convince him to leave this country.

Downstairs, I could hear people coming and going. Let their celebrations continue, I thought. I felt sad when I thought of Ali coming back to the office in defeat. How excited and happy he had been. He had been sure of success. He had spoken often of running into the streets to hoist the flag of victory, of bringing comfort to his uncle's heart by breaking the symbols of His Majesty's power. How could he confront his mother now, in this moment of defeat? They should have won. What is the point if the powerful side keeps winning? I continued to sit there in my room, in solidarity with the defeated Ali rather than with the victorious Taya Ghar.

Shahbaz called again. I didn't pick up at first because I thought he was going to scold me for not turning up at work. But he called again and again and I realized that it must be something important. He was calling from his own mobile phone.

'So you must be getting all the news?' he said in a soft voice.

'No, anything in particular?' I asked, surprised.

'Sameera, I thought you guys in Taya Ghar would hear the news first. In fact I was only calling to confirm.'

'Tell me what the matter is. I have no idea,' I said.

'Not confirmed, but I heard some sad news. Seven people

were killed in the shooting at the Square of Pearls. One might be our Hasan.'

'Hasan? Which Hasan?' My voice was trembling.

'Our Hasan, who else?'

'Oh no . . .' I screamed.

'Don't tell anybody. This is not yet confirmed. Why don't you check with your taya, he probably has more accurate news. And if you hear anything, let me know.' Shahbaz's voice was also shaky.

They had always shared a special friendship, Hasan and Shahbaz. In the arguments in Cattle Class Mercedes, Hasan would always come to Shahbaz's rescue. 'That cannot be our Hasan,' I tried to comfort him. In truth, I was trying to comfort myself.

It was in the newsroom, more than Cattle Class, that I got to know Hasan who was our Arabic translator. We had sympathized with each other and shared each other's fury at all the news reports we had to throw in the wastebasket because we were not allowed to broadcast the truth.

He hadn't even participated that much in the protests. When everyone else went, he too had gone a couple of times. Compared to Ali's zeal, Hasan was practically indifferent. There was no chance that he would have ended up there last night. It just could not be our Hasan who had died.

I called Ali. But his mobile was switched off. I called Salman, my String Walkers friend. But I got a recorded message that he was doing a live show and in case of emergency, callers should contact the studio.

I went downstairs. There were quite a lot of people I didn't know. They must have come to celebrate the military's victory, I thought. Now Taya Ghar would wake up from its slumber. Everyone loved winners. But neither taya nor baba were there. I was sad that even now they were prisoners of their jobs. It had been days since baba had left. So many days and nights of hard work in the street, fighting – who knew if he was eating food, getting any rest. I wanted to see my baba then. If only he would return right away.

I ignored all the guests and went to Aisha auntie's room to talk about Hasan. As soon as she saw me, her face darkened. But I started talking anyway. 'Auntie, you all wasted a day of mine. At least in the studio I could have figured out what was going on around the City. Did you hear about the shootings in the Square of Pearls? Did bhupo say anything?' I asked.

'Who told you?' she asked.

'Shahbaz called from the studio just now. You remember Hasan, one of the studio guys. Shahbaz thought Hasan might have been at the Square of Pearls. Allah, I hope not. He was such a nice guy, auntie.'

'Yes, yes . . . something seems to have happened there. No one knows who . . . what . . . Anyway, don't sit here. Go upstairs and if I hear anything, I'll tell you.'

I thought she was saying that because there were so many strangers about. 'Okay, make sure to tell me as soon as you hear anything,' I told her and went back up.

I switched on the TV. They were broadcasting live from His Majesty's palace where national leaders and foreign diplomats were lining up to congratulate him. Some of them hugged His Majesty. Others kissed him. Yet others were laying their swords at his feet. And some prostrated and proclaimed their fealty. There were leaders there who had even contested in the protesters' elections and had supported the protests. I stared at the TV wondering at the breadth of human opportunism. It was like watching a comedy show. Shahbaz called a few times to ask if I had heard anything but I had no news for him.

After a while, something unusual happened. All the women of the house – Sippy auntie, Aisha auntie, all my chachis and Farhana came to my room. 'Why are you all here?' I asked. But no one answered. Aisha auntie came and sat with me on the bed and grasped my hand in hers. Then they started weeping. And though I didn't know why, I found myself crying too.

Baba

They told me that baba had been slightly wounded. They asked me to get ready to go to the hospital. They continued to cry.

It was as if a spark of fire fell on my skin. What happened? When? Where? Why didn't anyone tell me this before? They had no answers.

Since I had got ready for the studio earlier in the day, I went downstairs right away. Khalid chacha was waiting in his car. Sippy auntie and Aisha auntie got into the car with me. The others got into bhupo's car.

My heart beat painfully, eager to see baba. The vehicles seemed to be moving at snail's pace. The red lights went on forever. The soldiers at the checkposts seemed to stop people for no reason. I was annoyed at everyone and everything on the street. I have to see baba. I have to see baba. I have to see baba. My mind would not be at peace till I saw baba.

But our vehicles did not go to the main door of the hospital, instead they went to the mortuary gate. A huge crowd of our friends and family members had gathered there, including lots of police officers. Fear crept up my spine, like a little yellow lizard. It pressed its feet into my head. I was shattered. Taya peeled off from the crowd and came towards us. I felt as if I was standing at the edge of a cliff. Taya looked many years older. He hugged me. I tried hard not to but a sob escaped me.

'Do not cry,' taya told me, hugging me closer to him. 'You are a Khan woman. War is what our family does. When our warriors die, we give them a funeral that honours their bravery. They cannot take our tears. My brother was a brave man. His daughter should be brave too.'

Taya took me inside. I could feel thousands of eyes upon us and I pressed my tears down, strangled them in my throat, choked them back inside. For the sake of the spectators, I became a brave Khan woman.

Someone from the crowd shouted, 'Bolo Takbir ... Allahu Akbar.' The crowd took it up. 'Bolo Takbir ... Allahu Akbar ...'

'No tears,' taya reminded me again.

Baba was lying under a white sheet in that room. The air smelled of camphor and alcoholic spirits. It took every bit of courage in my bones to look at baba's face. Was that really my baba? What I saw was an old man's face. There was a stubble of dry brown hair on that face. His forehead was bruised and there was blood-soaked cotton in his nose and ears.

When we were children we loved playing with the wart on my baba's face, right next to his left eyebrow. That was how I identified him. If that wart hadn't been there on that face, I would still not have believed it. Baba was lying with his eyes partly closed, as if asleep. Later I wondered if he was unrecognizable because the tragedies of the last one week had scarred his face, changed its contours, stubbled its smoothness.

I shut my eyes for a moment. In that one moment, I saw in my mind a thousand expressions. His smile, his anger, his sympathy, his sadness, his love. I had never seen baba so clearly as then.

I bent down and kissed his face.

That was not customary. Everyone, including taya, was startled. A senior police officer came forward and escorted me and taya away. No one seemed to hear me begging to stay for a few more minutes. They led us through the crowds and took us to the car. Taya stayed with me in the car. And then suddenly he, who had been giving me courage and comfort till then, burst into tears. I fell into his arms and started weeping.

For a long time both of us sat in the car, feeling empty inside out. After a while, our radio team approached the car. Rajeevan sir, Fathima madam, Imthiaz sir, Shahbaz, Viju Prasad, Sheetal, Meera Maskan, Sharon, Minesh and Sheela Garments, they were all there. They stood next to the car. I was grateful that they did not try to comfort me. But then other friends and distant family members started approaching the car and looking at me through the window as if I was an object of pity. Their looks were unbearable. I closed my eyes and sat in my own darkness. Some soldiers and policemen eventually asked them to leave. Only Sippy auntie and Khalid chacha remained. Taya told them to take me home and opened the door of the car.

I held his hand. 'We must take baba home. He always wanted to be laid to rest in that soil,' I told him. But taya gently separated my hand from his and went away with the police officers without meeting my eyes.

Unfulfilled Dreams

Baba had always dreamed of being buried in Faisalabad. He would talk about it whenever he came home on holiday. 'I am going to return here one of these days when you kids are no longer fledglings. I want to spend the rest of my life here in peace. This is my soil. This is where I want to finish my life.' Perhaps that is why baba alone, of all his brothers in the City, never applied for citizenship. When I got my job, baba was happy. Because now he could return home to Faisalabad that much earlier.

But that dream of baba's was ruthlessly dismissed. He was buried in the City. I felt as if I had sacrificed his dream. I imagined him crying from under the mud, 'Beti, even though you were right here, you could not manage to do this much for me.' It messed up my brain. Allah decides when to take your life. But surely a human has the right to decide where to be buried. Baba didn't get even that much.

That was my fault. Would baba curse me? I felt as if I had been betrayed. My anger was bigger than my grief. That evening I walked into taya's room, ignoring all the guests, and quarrelled with him.

But taya had a hundred justifications. 'Beti,' he said calmly, 'I did know of that dream of his. Perhaps it is not just his dream. Don't we all dream of returning to that soil? But shouldn't we surrender to God's will? Our religion tells us that burials should take place wherever the death takes place and as soon as possible after the death. That custom is bigger than one person's dream. Also, my child, he is your father and my brother. But he is also a policeman who lost his life fighting for this country. And when the government wants to give him an official funeral with all the honours, who am I to say no? I see it as a reward for his life and death.'

I knew that whatever the religion said, funerals could wait a bit, if necessary. Even Prophet Muhammad's body was buried after one and a half days. So that was not the reason, I speculated. Taya and the others were citizens of this country. They had no intention of ever returning. This is where they would live till the end of their lives. Perhaps they had selfishly decided that their brother too should stay with them, here in this country. Mad with grief, I told as much to taya.

'Beti, please don't be so cruel to me. I cannot bear this any more. I am more shattered than you are.'

If Aisha auntie hadn't come and gently taken me to my room, I would have continued to wound taya with my words. He was responsible for everything. He was the one who had brought baba here. He was the one who got baba into police work. And then he was the reason baba got promoted from Nathoor to an armed policeman. Wasn't it taya who had sent baba to the protesters' battlefields? Yes, it was all taya's fault and only his fault.

That night I found yet another reason to blame taya. I was lying in bed crying and remembering baba when I thought of ma, Saima and Sameer. How could I have forgotten them till then? Did they know what had happened? Or was taya hiding the news from them? I kicked up a big fuss at Taya Ghar, demanding that I talk to them right away. Taya came out of his room and told me that they knew everything and that I must not call right now.

What unfortunates they were. Ma would not see her husband's face one last time and my siblings would not see their father's face one last time. That too was taya's fault. He had been too busy upholding customs and beliefs to think of their sorrow.

Baba had often dreamed of bringing ma here on a visiting visa and taking her sightseeing around the country. But that had been impossible on his meagre salary. 'Now that you are here and you have a job, we should get your ma here. If you ask, she'll come. We have to show her that Faisalabad is not the beginning and the end of the universe,' he used to tell me. Another dream that was never realized. Some people's dreams are like that. They are just meant to be taken out for an airing every now and then, not to be fulfilled, even by accident.

That night, two lines from a poem kept ringing in my head. Baba used to recite these words often.

Maut par haq hai
Lekin kafan par shaq hai
(Death is certain, but a shroud is not)

Ruined Memorials

Beyond my balcony, the City was celebrating its victory. The streets that had been noisy for so long with slogans now became noisy with victory songs. There was lots of honking and flying flags and shouts of 'Long Live His Majesty'. From my bed I could see flowers of light and colour blooming in the sky as firecrackers were set off. It was as if all of the City was mocking me. I resented myself for ever coming to this country.

The friends and relations had all left Taya Ghar. The house was now an island of loneliness. Everyone disappeared into their rooms. Aisha auntie did not want to leave me alone and was sleeping in my room. I lay awake in the dark, next to her.

'Bhupoma, are you asleep?' I asked her.

'No, dear. What is the matter?'

'There's a pain in my chest . . . I feel as if I have no one.'

'You have us.'

'I want to talk to ma . . .'

'At this time of the night?'

'Yes.'

'Why, my dear? Neither of you will be able to even speak. All you can do is cry.'

'At least I could hear her cry.'

'Don't do it, my dear. Even if we have to cry a lot, it is best not to make others cry.'

'I want to cry.'

She hugged me. I wept in her arms.

My memories kept me awake for a long time. Whenever I closed my eyes, I saw baba before my eyes. He seemed to be weeping and reproaching me, 'You should have done more.' That thought haunted me.

I was jolted out of sleep the next morning by a huge sound from outside. It was as if a small earthquake was travelling down the street. When I hurried to the balcony, I saw a long row of cranes, diggers, bulldozers, trucks and pick-ups, being escorted by military vehicles.

It was Aisha auntie who told me to check the breaking news on TV. The government was going to demolish the Square of Pearls. They wanted to erase any memory or symbol of the revolution.

The Square had been built several years ago for an international conference in the City. Then it became a symbol of the country itself. It appeared on stamps, flags and banners. Perhaps that is why the protesters themselves had chosen the square. To capture the Square of Pearls was to capture the country itself.

In four hours, the Square was no more. On TV, we could see every detail of the demolition. Diggers and cranes were removing every trace of it. Soon the Square of Pearls with its decades of history was nothing but an empty field.

By noon, the police were all over the highway. Senior police officers' cars were speeding up and down. It was clear that something important was going to happen. What were they up to now? After a while, a motorcade of covered cars and tanks appeared at one end of the highway. In the very centre, His Majesty stood in a car next to a tall flag. Perhaps this was the first time he had ever appeared in front of the people of this country. The majority of citizens had only ever seen him on TV. And in fact today as well that was the case. The highway was empty though he kept waving and smiling and kissing the air as if a sea of spectators were cheering him on. Had he gone mad with triumph?

The motorcade ended in the rubble that was the Square of Pearls. His Majesty hoisted the flag there and made his victory speech, which was broadcast live on national TV. 'The Square of Pearls was once the symbol of our dreams. Unfortunately it later became the symbol of hatred, division and sedition. No longer! The country is going to erase those terrible memories. From today, we are a new people.'

Then there were thank yous. To the police, the army and the foreign military for smoking out the protesters. To the patriotic citizens who had backed him.

Then it was time for the traditional dance with members of his family – a dance similar to the one we had seen on TV the day the City was rioting.

The next day, the police began their real hunt.

Crossing the River of Grief

I didn't learn about it until much later. The very next day I went to Faisalabad. I could not live for another day without

208

seeing ma, Saima and Sameer. Taya agreed. 'Your ma won't be happy till she sees you. Go stay with them. You can return after they are back to normal.'

I was not sure if the studio would let me go for that long. But taya offered to speak to Imthiaz sir for me. 'And if that doesn't work, just let the job go. We can always find another job. By then you'll get your certificates,' he said.

But I couldn't imagine a life without radio any more. So I made taya call Rajeevan sir and Imthiaz sir. They both assured me that I could go for as long as I liked.

So I went home for what I thought would be a month at the most. But when I got home, I found that ma was completely shattered. In fact, at times she wouldn't even believe that baba was dead. Often I would hear her saying anxiously, 'He will be home soon.' She started slipping more and more into a delusional state.

I had to postpone my return. My co-workers and listeners stopped expecting me to return at all.

Even in her nightmares ma hadn't imagined him leaving us so soon. After all she had had no chance to see his corpse or attend his funeral. If only they had let me bring his body home and bury it here. Then at least she could have experienced the grief in its entirety. Perhaps that would have helped her recover. But for ma, baba's death was a folk tale that had happened somewhere far away from her. She refused to believe it. You have to swim across the river of grief, shore to shore. It's painful but if you don't, you are doomed to sink in it.

The Unforgivable Sin

Yesterday, when I was returning from the souk, I ran into our former receptionist at the studio, Laila. She used to be a chatterbox, always laughing, teasing and full of stories about Shia greatness. But now she was like a faded version of herself. Laila was one of the thousands who had been fired from offices around the country for protesting. There were so many in our own studio like her. Instead of Hasan, we now had a new translator. Just as Shahbaz had suspected, Hasan was one of the seven people who were shot to death in the Square of Pearls. To this day no one knows how he ended up there.

Instead of Yunus, we had a new driver. Instead of Laila and Khadija at the reception, we had two women from the Philippines now. One day I went by Ali's maintenance office. Instead of Ali, Abdullah Janahi and Muneer Gazi, now there were three military staff members in charge of maintenance. They had two Indians with them as well. From the security box at the gate to the desks inside, there were more and more military staff members everywhere. Only John Maschinas remained in the administration and there were rumours that he too was on his way out. We had imagined this protest changing the country. But all it had done was change the lives of some for the worse.

As soon as she saw me, Laila burst into tears. She was actually a simple young woman. In the heat of the protests, she had got carried away. When all her friends went protesting, she too had gone. It was like going to a party, as far as she was concerned. Left to herself, she wasn't particularly interested in overthrowing the government or participating in seditious activities. In fact, most of the protesters were in the same category. But when disciplinary action was taken, they were also included. 'Government orders.' Our management shrugged it off.

Laila was indeed a devout Shia. We only found out that day when we saw her kicking Yunus. But she probably had not imagined that her devoutness would end up getting her fired.

'I am just an ordinary girl, Sameera,' she said. 'I just have ordinary dreams and all I want is to enjoy my life without too much hassle. And most of my girlfriends who took part in the protests, they were also like that. What I really want in my life is a nice house. I used to joke often that I would happily be some old man's second wife or mistress as long as I got a house in the bargain. You know those ads you see on the side of the road for houses and apartments? Those advertisement houses were the houses of my dreams. I would think, dear God, who gets lucky enough to live in these houses? One day I asked baba, why can't we live in a nice house like that? And baba told me that it was pointless to even dream of it. Even if we worked hard for three generations, the likes of us would not be able to afford one of those houses.

'Those houses are not that amazing, you know. They are just ordinary nice houses. I felt ashamed of myself that I was too poor to afford a house like that, a basic house. Then I became jealous of those who could choose to buy one of those houses. I started feeling that they were getting rich off us. The reason they could afford those houses was because I could not. And that anger and despair led me to the protests. All I wanted was a nice house of my own.'

Then she held my hands and cried. 'It's all because I am a Shia. I used to be so proud of it. But now I am afraid to tell anyone. It's a sin to be a Shia in this country. An unforgivable sin. How terrible it is to be persecuted in the name of one's faith. Never mind myself. I am mostly worried about my daughter. I don't know if you know, though we live in the same country, Shias and Sunnis have different traditions, when it comes to our clothes and language. How much can you hide it? My seven-year-old daughter does not want to go to school any more. The Sunni kids won't play with her. And that's not the worst part. She now tries to imitate the Sunni kids. She wants to dress like them, talk like them. Who are we any more in this country? I didn't know that we would pay such a high price for this protest. I feel like a snake that has been beaten just enough to keep hurting, but not enough to die.'

Man of the Match

One evening I was sitting on my balcony playing the guitar that baba had given me when Aisha auntie told me that I had some visitors. 'For me?' I was surprised. Who would come to Taya Ghar to see me, so late in the day? I went downstairs, wondering.

It had been days since I had been downstairs. As soon as I got home, I would go to my room and shut the door. If I got bored, I would hang out on my balcony and watch the streets. Or I would go for a walk in the souk. I kept Taya Ghar at a distance.

That was not without reason. Taya Ghar was not too happy about my return. I learned this from what they said to ma on the phone when I was visiting her. 'This girl keeps roaming around the City with young men of her fancy. She has brought shame on all of us. It is hard to control her, especially now without her own baba. Don't send her back,' they said. Then they played on ma's loneliness. 'You need someone to take care of you. Find her a job there, that's best.'

In fact, I too had decided to stay back home with ma after seeing her go to pieces. But then, one day, Aisha auntie called me in secret. 'You have to come back,' she said. 'Whatever happens, make sure you return. If you don't, the loss will be yours.' That's when I started suspecting something was afoot. But even then I didn't guess what the loss would be.

So one day I returned here without asking anyone's permission. Even ma only half agreed with my plan. And only after I got back did I realize what was going on. The government had declared a huge reward recognizing baba's service to the country. The amount could change my family's life. But someone at Taya Ghar had decided that the reward was meant to honour not just baba but all the men of the Khan family. Bhupo and Sippy auntie were the main proponents of this theory. But Aisha auntie knew the truth and that is why she had called me secretly. She guessed that if I was not around, baba's brothers would divide up the price of his blood and we would get only a small part of the reward. I learned later that there had been many loud arguments at Taya Ghar about this. Even taya was silenced by Sippy auntie's money-hungry justifications. And that is how I learned that even brotherly love disappears when money is at stake.

Taya Ghar had not expected me to return. They had been sure that once they convinced ma of my shameless ways, I would be on a tight leash back home. And no one told me anything about a reward even several days after my arrival. But as baba's heir, only I had the right to accept it. If I had not been there, someone else could have. In the end, I had to ask taya. 'Yes, I was going to bring it up. They are processing all the paperwork for that. We have to go get it.' Taya's reply was evasive. But Sippy auntie did not waste any time on diplomacy. 'You may be the one receiving it. But this is a reward for all the men of the family. And you have to see it that way.' Javed, if you had heard her rationalizations, you might have slapped her cheek. In fact, I almost raised my hand. But I held back because I remembered her age and all the favours she had done for me and baba over the years. According to her, when a cricket player wins the Man of the Match trophy, the prize is divided equally among all the players.

'This is not some trophy my baba got for playing cricket. This is the price of his life. So please stop eyeing it and please don't think you'll get a piece of it,' I said before leaving taya's room. I didn't even really want that money. If they had asked affectionately, if they had needed it, I would have shared it with his brothers. But that's not what they did. They tried to elbow us out of it completely. And I could not bow down to such greed.

And so I became an island within Taya Ghar. No one

would talk to me. Though no one said it out loud, it was clear that they wanted me to move elsewhere. In the kitchen, they stopped counting me for meals. Can anything hurt more?

I, too, wanted to move out. But Khalid chacha and Aisha auntie told me that if I didn't stick it out there, things might not go well. There is no bigger tragedy than becoming a stranger to your own family.

So that was the situation when my visitors arrived. I went downstairs wondering who it could be.

Visitors

I could never have predicted it – my guests that evening were the String Walkers. I was delighted to see them. I felt myself blooming into a happiness I had not known lately. Memories of our musical evenings came rushing back. For a few moments, all the loneliness and disappointment I had been feeling melted. I thought that all the divisions that had surfaced in the last few months had destroyed our group. But the power of music had brought them together again. Like the strings of a guitar, they were of one mind and one sound. That was not the only reason. I was also happy that they had come searching for me, even though I hadn't really been a member for very long. I had become a pariah in Taya Ghar but I still had other friends. I felt proud.

Nazar, Ifran, Salman and Roger greeted me with big smiles. Farah and Sophia hugged me. I didn't know how to react – it was as if God himself had come visiting. I invited

215

them into the living room and went to get something for them to drink. I made some noise in the kitchen – why not let Taya Ghar know that even I had guests. They expressed condolences about baba's death and regretted that they could not come and see me then. For a long time, we sat there talking.

Even amidst all that happiness, I felt sad about Ali's absence.

'If only Ali was here,' I said. 'I miss him so much. Is he still upset about the protests?'

My friends looked at me in shock. But no one said anything. Later Ali came up again and again in our conversation. Even then they did not tell me anything. But finally Salman said, 'Really Sameera, are you joking? Or do you really not know what happened?'

'What??'

'About Ali.'

'No? No one told me anything. What happened to him? I went home to Pakistan a couple of days after baba's death. And since then I have been really out of touch with news here.'

'And no one told you when you came back?'

'No. I guess he lost his job because of the protests? I tried calling him a few times but didn't get through.'

'He is in prison.'

'Prison? Why?' I asked fearfully.

They looked at each other. 'It was a murder,' Salman broke the silence finally. 'We thought you knew all about it. But if you don't know . . . we'll come back another time.'

They stood up. It was as if they all wanted to escape from me as soon as possible.

'Please don't leave. Tell me what happened. I don't know anything. Please,' I begged.

But they left, one by one, without listening to my pleas. 'Farah, I am already going mad with anxiety. I cannot bear this. Please, whatever it is, won't you tell me?' I stopped Farah.

'Ask someone at home . . . they can tell you.' She tried to evade me.

'No Farah. Either they don't know or they don't want me to know. Otherwise they would have told me by now.'

Farah was silent for a moment. Then she told me, 'Ali. Ali is responsible for your baba's death.'

Traitor

All through that night I tossed and turned in bed, my pain stuck in my throat. My baba didn't just die an accidental death, he was murdered. And his murderer was my best friend, Ali. But why? And how? How come I didn't know any of this earlier? I had become an outsider in Taya Ghar. So they didn't tell me. But why did Aisha auntie and Khalid chacha hide this from me? The questions simmered inside me. I was being duped by everyone, as if I were a prostitute forced to go back into the street again and again. I decided that now I had to know everything. I wanted to clear the fog that lay above the truth. As soon as it was dawn, I went to taya's room and knocked on the door even though he was sleeping. Sippy auntie came to the door, panicking. She was not too happy to see me but I ignored that and said that I needed to talk to taya urgently. 'Go wait in the office room. He'll meet you there when he is awake,' she said. I thought I would have to wait forever, but perhaps taya overheard us. He got ready quickly and joined me there.

'What's the matter, beti? Why are you up so early?'

'How was my baba killed?' I asked without beating around the bush.

'So that's what you want to know so early this morning? You already know how – he was killed in the protests.' His answer was indifferent.

'Who killed my baba?'

'Traitors, who else?'

'Does the murderer have a name?'

'The name is irrelevant, beti. Traitors are traitors. Even identifying them by name is a crime.'

'But I need to know the name,' I insisted.

'I heard you had some guests last night. Who were they?' Taya shot back a question.

'Some friends of mine,' I said.

'What brought them here?'

'I don't know. They didn't say much.'

'They didn't give you the answer to your question?'

'Yes, they did. I am asking you to confirm what they said.'

'Do you think they would lie to you?'

'Are you sure that it was Ali who killed my baba?'

'I don't know if his name is Ali. All I know is that he was

a Second Class. A traitor who participated in the protests and tried to overthrow the government.'

'Everyone in this house knows Ali. And taya, you know all about our friendship. If you are sure he killed my baba, why didn't you tell me so? Don't I have the right to know? What crime have I committed against Taya Ghar that you would hide this from me?'

Sippy auntie had been eavesdropping on us from behind the door and as soon as I asked this, she clomped into the room like a wounded pig.

'You were upset because we put an end to your little love story with that fellow and so you asked him to kill our brother . . .'

'Auntie! Don't think you can say anything you want because baba is no more.' I leaped to my feet.

'I am not afraid of telling the truth. Our brother was deliberately targeted and killed by that fellow.'

'Who is "that fellow" and who is this "brother" that you keep talking of? How can my baba be dearer to you than to me?'

'Oh, what a dear baba. Is that why you came running back here not even three months after he died, so you could flirt and philander with random men on the radio? The shame of it. We can no longer hold up our heads outside this house. Taya Ghar used to be a respected name in this city. You single-handedly destroyed it.'

'You have no other way of thinking, auntie, because your mind is so filthy. I am not going to talk to you any more. But taya, why didn't you tell me all this?'

'Because you don't deserve to know,' Sippy auntie interrupted us again.

All the rage inside me came rushing to my head. But luckily taya chided Sippy auntie and sent her away. Otherwise, she would have really got a tongue-lashing from this harami.

'Beti.' Taya was still very calm. He was serene as always, unshaken by the cold war in the house, my waking him up early, and the fight with Sippy auntie. 'It is best not to know some things. Not only is it useless to know, they will hurt us forever if we do know.'

'Yes, that would be fine if I didn't know anything at all. Then ignorance would be a protection. But to know bits and pieces . . . that's like walking around with an open wound. I couldn't sleep at all last night.'

'It was indeed your friend Ali who killed your baba. It was for your own good that we didn't tell you all the details, not because anyone here resents you. Don't give a second thought to all that Sippy auntie said. We all know she is a motormouth.'

'But why? And how? You have to tell me, taya. I have the right to know.'

'I don't know why. We are still investigating that. But if you insist on knowing how he died, all you have to do is search on YouTube. Someone has posted the video with the date of the murder.'

'YouTube? My baba's death is on YouTube? What are you saying, taya?'

'Yes, beti. You can search for it if you like. But with all my love, I would advise you not to.'

I ran to my room, switched on the computer and opened YouTube. I didn't have to search long before I found 'Live murder of a policeman'. It had 11 lakh views. Everyone, it seems, had seen it except me. What a world. Perhaps this is how we all live, surrounded by secrets whose existence we don't know of.

YouTube

I watched that video with brimming eyes. It was shot from the roof of a tall building or from a helicopter. The images were not very clear. First we saw a group of helmeted policemen running into a field with shields. They were shooting into the air and exploding tear gas. The video did not show who they were aiming at, but there were bottles, stones and tyres on fire flying towards the policemen. The police withdrew and returned. After this game had gone on for a while, a car sped into the midst of the policemen. Though they tried to stop it with bullets and tear gas, it kept zigzagging through them. All the policemen ran away to escape. But one of them fell. He struggled to get up and run for his life but the car kept hitting him and running over him as if the driver had gone mad.

I closed the window. I could not see any more. When I thought of the sheer pain my baba must have been in, in that moment, my chest throbbed. I sat with my eyes closed, sobbing, my head spinning. I got into bed and cowered under the blanket.

After a while, when my courage returned, I went back

and watched the video again. I still couldn't bear the horror and again ended up under the blanket. That's all I did that day. Each time I watched, I hoped that the video would magically change course. My baba would emerge alive from under the car. But each time, baba let me down and fell under those tyres. By evening I was exhausted. My body ached intensely and I felt cold. For a week I was sick with a terrible fever. Whether I was sleeping or awake, or half-conscious, the video kept playing in front of my eyes, with even more clarity than it had on YouTube.

Amidst all that, I had another thought. What was the proof that Ali drove that car? For that matter, who could prove that the fallen man was my baba? The images did not show either of their faces. So I refused to believe. Someone had dragged Ali into this deliberately to implicate him. Ali was not capable of killing someone so ruthlessly. And surely this story of my baba dying under the wheels of a car was meant to dishonour him. My baba was a Khan. He must have died a warrior's death, taking a bullet in a face-to-face confrontation. Feverishly I tried to convince myself of all this.

But I couldn't deny the reality of that car. When the camera zoomed in, I could see the sticker on its rear window, the grey seat cover, the extra fitting next to its number plate, the dented bumper. I knew all these little details. Ali had given me many rides in his car.

Part 6

The Vulture and the Hare

Walking the Streets

When I got up from my bed after the fever subsided, there was no returning to the old Sameera. I was constantly haunted by how baba was killed like a street dog. And by my dear friend. He had probably never seen my baba and he hadn't imagined that the man he was killing could be Sameera's father. But Ali knew the pain of losing someone to such a gruesome death. He had seen his own brother dying like that. How could that Ali be the instrument of the same kind of death? Had he forgotten all his memories, experiences and dreams when he set out to kill? Or did he want someone else to feel the pain that he had carried around in his heart?

Like wild bees that had built a hive inside my head, these questions kept buzzing inside me. Whether I was walking or lying down, facing the microphone at the studio or riding in Cattle Class, they gnawed at me. One day, when my thoughts were completely unbearable, I slung my guitar over my shoulders and went for a walk. I was walking aimlessly, simply glad to bear the heaviness of baba's love for me. But my feet took me to the backyard of the Starbucks where

String Walkers used to meet. I had never gone there on my own. I didn't even know the way there. Whenever I went there with a driver, I would give wrong directions. But that day, my feet knew the way somehow. Perhaps it was my unconscious mind that guided me there. Of course there was no one from String Walkers there. I ordered a coffee and started playing my guitar. I played baba's favourite song, 'Papa kehte hain'. With the song came my tears. But I could also feel the buzzing bees in my head disappear into silence. I could sense peace filling the space they left behind.

When I was about to leave, an old man who was sitting in a corner called out to me. In fact, I had seen him before. During our meetings at that cafe, he could often be seen sitting in a corner with his eyes glued to his book. None of us had imagined that he was actually listening to us. But as we talked, it became clear that he knew all of us, each of our favourite songs and what kind of music we specialized in. Who knew that we had a silent admirer?

'You walked here all alone. How about we walk back together?' he said.

'But it's a long way. Will you be able to . . .?'

'So what if I fall down and die along the way. At least I will walk till then. Let's be optimistic!'

I hadn't thought of what I had implied. 'No, no, I was not suggesting that you are too old.'

'Never mind that. Walk or not?' he insisted.

'Let's walk,' I said.

He put away his book and got up. I slung the guitar around my shoulder. We walked. By then it was dark and some of the neon lamps on the street were not working. But the headlights from the vehicles on the street gave us enough light. In the distance, we could still hear the ambulances. That reminded me that the City was not yet completely back to normal. Even now, there were isolated incidents of violence. A petrol bomb aimed at a passing police car. A burning tyre on the road or a smashed light signal. They were mostly the pranks of ten-and twelve-year-olds. The government had silenced one generation of youth in one stroke by suppressing the protests, but the generation that would take their place was already brimming with anger.

A few patrolling police vehicles passed us. They seemed to be eyeing us suspiciously. But somehow I did not feel uncomfortable walking with a stranger. Instead, I felt as secure as if I was with my baba.

During our walk, my new friend started telling me a story. 'Every day the village children would play in front of the mosque and make a mess. The imam got tired of this and one day, to distract them, he said, "I hear there is a huge monster in the village river." The kids ran off yelling, "Monster in the river, monster in the river!", convinced that it was the truth because after all, the imam said so. When the villagers heard the children yelling, they too joined the race to the river. As they passed the mosque, they yelled to the imam, "Did you hear, there's a monster in the river." The imam was laughing at first. But after hearing a lot of people yell, he started thinking, "Perhaps a monster is indeed floating in the river?" After some time he completely forgot that he had made up the monster to trick the children. He got out and ran to the river. It's human nature, isn't it, to run to the river to see the monster we made up,' he said.

I smiled and didn't say anything.

'I told you this story because that's what Ali did. He ran to the river to see the monster that he had made up.'

'Ali? How do you know Ali?'

'You were new to String Walkers. I knew all the old members. In fact, it was I who pointed out that cafe as a good place for them to practice.'

I thought of all the stray comments I had made at String Walkers about this old man in the corner with his book. None of them, not even Ali, had told me then that they knew him.

'It is not just from the cafe that I know Ali,' he continued. 'Do you remember going to see Ali's uncle? I am a friend of his. We were neighbours in prison the first three years. In those days, we killed time by telling each other our life stories. Then they moved me to a cell further away. And after ten years, they released me. Ali's uncle had to stay there for eight years more.'

I began getting nervous. So he wasn't just a stranger who had admired our music while reading his book. I was walking with someone who knew more about me than he should. Random strangers are not as dangerous as someone who has been collecting information secretly. What was his aim? I was filled with a trepidation I could not have expressed. I just wanted to get home.

'It's very late. I think the walk home will take a long time. Shall we take a taxi?' I asked.

'Never mind how late it is. I intend to see you to the doorstep before I die.' He laughed. 'We have a lot more to talk about.' He continued to walk.

228

'Ali's baba and I were teachers in the same school. He taught Arabic and I taught science. We used to see each other a lot and talk about everything under the sun. He was brave to a fault. That's the kind of man the police took away one day for no reason. That's the kind of man who was never allowed to return to his family. Maybe Ali told you some of this? He grew up bearing the brunt of not having a father. The world he saw through his eyes was very different from the one you or I see.'

'Why are you telling me all this now?' I asked him angrily. 'I didn't bring up Ali.'

'You know, I enjoy your show on the radio a lot. And I can tell that you have lost your old zest for life. Sometimes, you get tongue-tied, the words don't come out. I can tell that your heart is elsewhere. Am I right?'

'Well, of course my heart is elsewhere. You can say that ever so casually. But you know, I lost my father. You may not understand what that means, but surely Ali did. Before he killed my baba, did he think for a minute – perhaps this man has a daughter somewhere.' Even the blood in my veins was hot with anger now.

'That's why I told you the story of the imam. Poor Ali, he is an idiot who ran to the river to see the monster of his own fiction. If we don't see where a person is coming from, then all our education and experience is useless.'

By then we were approaching Taya Ghar.

'I have more to tell you. But our walk was so short. When can I see you again?' he asked.

I was silent. My indifference was obvious.

'My dear child, if you want to solve a problem, first

you have to accept that it is a problem. Then you have to understand it. You have to relate to it and forgive it . . .'

I walked into Taya Ghar without listening to the rest.

'I will be in my seat at the cafe every evening. Whenever you want to see me again, you will find me there,' he called after me.

Fictions

'You will never go visit that old man who justified what Ali did,' I admonished myself many times. But still, I couldn't get his words out of my mind. He was right that my heart was elsewhere. It was burning with questions. I could not concentrate on anything else. My live shows had become tame, and the only reason no one at work had brought it up was out of their fondness for me. But the old man had spoken so frankly. I had to accept the reality, as he had said. Why live inside a false dream?

So this then was the reality. My father did not die the brave death a Khan warrior should have. He died like a street dog. He was killed by my best friend, Ali. Fine, I accept this cold reality. But still, I could not forgive it. He did not commit a crime that could be forgiven so easily. Had it been an accident, perhaps I could have forgiven him. Or if he was one of those who could not understand the depth of what he did. But to commit a crime even while knowing the exact pain it would cause. Such a crime cannot be forgiven, even if committed by a loved one. That's why I had no sympathy for Ali who had killed baba and for Taya Ghar which had put a price on his life.

My radio performances continued to be soulless. When I was at home, I shut myself up in my room, slowly going mad. But one day I was sitting in the park opposite our flat when I saw the old man again. This time, he was wearing exercise clothes and running. I feared that he might fall down and die on the way home, so old and tired did he look. Still he ran. I was amazed by his attitude. There was so much optimism in his running as if he fully expected that there were many years ahead of him. I could have avoided him then. But I got up and approached him. He stopped running and greeted me. Then he invited me to go on a walk with him. I couldn't say no.

He had another story this time. 'I have a granddaughter. Her name is Amina. Like all children, she prefers me to her own father. And of course, I fully reciprocate her affection. You know, we always love our grandchildren more than we love our children. One day, she came to me and said in all seriousness, "Dada, did you know that eating onions makes you beautiful? You should have eaten more onions when you were a child."'

I burst out laughing.

'Someone had told her this story and she became a complete believer. Whenever salad is served, she has to have all the onions. Even if we are eating dal, she wants onions in it. And she won't eat biriyani without onions. Her whole life is full of onions now. And I didn't discourage her. I thought – she is a small child, why not go along? Every day she came to me at least four or five times to tell me why onions are so great. And now, after hearing this so often, I have started believing that onions can make you beautiful.

'She also believes that eating lots of fish makes you a good swimmer. And so she eats a lot of fish. And even though I know this is not true, I too believe in it. In fact, I imagine that I must have eaten lots of fish and hence, I am a good swimmer.'

'I don't understand why you are telling me all these stories. If it is just to kill time while walking, then yes, I am enjoying them. But if not, then I am afraid . . .'

'I just told you how a four-year-old made me believe things by repeating them again and again. So imagine the kind of things we would believe if smooth-talking politicians and religious leaders kept talking to us, insisting that they alone have the truth. Our biases and beliefs have a lot to do with what we grow up hearing. And that's what happened to Ali.'

'You are still justifying Ali? Maybe you have seen the YouTube video in which Ali kills my baba? Did you notice how he hit my baba again and again?'

'I am glad you mentioned it, my child. I have seen the video, not once, but a thousand times. And I, too, wondered what was going on in his mind at that moment. The answer I found is that religion had poisoned his mind entirely.

'He grew up in a family without men because they were all in prison. He grew up wild without anyone to show him the way. He learned about life from his friends on the street and about religion from madrasas full of hate. When we were young, we had good leaders. They taught us to fight a good fight. They taught us that anger, resentment and the desire for revenge would not take us very far. We learned to use our judgement, we learned to be impartial. Our generation knew how to spend ten or twelve or twenty years in jail but emerge with our spirits intact. But Ali's generation grew up differently. Their leaders taught them to throw a bomb at the slightest provocation. Like a child insisting that onions make you beautiful, Ali's leaders kept telling lies till they became true. And like a child convinced that eating fish makes you a good swimmer, he grew up thinking that killing a policeman would help overthrow the government. That is why he behaved the way he did.

'Perhaps when he was hitting your father he was remembering how, centuries ago, when the Prophet's grandson Hussain was killed in Karbala, the soldiers of Ubaidullah rode their horses over the corpse again and again. In that one mad moment, he must have been trying to avenge crimes committed against Shias by Mu'awiya, Yazidi, Ubaidullah, Marwan, Shamir . . . Keeping ancient hatreds alive and passing them down through generations . . . sometimes that's what religion does. And every year Ashura reminds us of those stories.'

There was truth in what he said. I had myself seen how much pride Ali took in his heritage, how loyal he was to his faith and people.

'Here's the funny thing, daughter. Perhaps you didn't notice this. Up until that scene, your father was the attacking vulture and Ali was the hare. Till that moment, your father had a gun in his hands. He was wearing a

233

shield to protect himself from stones. He was one of that big group of soldiers and policemen who rushed into the crowd of unarmed protesters, like hunting dogs. Perhaps he was one of those who had fired shots into the crowd. And maybe Ali rushed into the fray hoping to save at least one of those innocents. But the moment your baba lost his gun, he turned into a hare and Ali became the vulture. Life goes on beyond the scene on YouTube. Both Ali and your baba were prey – one was the prey of death and the other the prey of the law. So who was the real vulture? Who did, Ali and your baba fight for? What did they get out of it?

'My baba was just a coolie policeman. He didn't shoot anyone out of hatred or resentment. All he did was carry out an order. There's a difference between what he did and what Ali did.'

'No! Ali was also merely a coolie, carrying out orders. Maybe his orders came from politicians who make tools out of young men. Or maybe they came from a religious leader promising heaven. Or maybe it was his own mental delusion in which all policemen were enemies. The day you understand this about Ali, you will finally be able to move on,' he said.

'I will try,' I said. Whatever.

'You are not just a creature of your emotions. You are an intelligent young woman. So don't just say you will try, to fob me off. Make a real effort,' he went on.

'I should leave now. I haven't told anyone at home where I am,' I said.

'You are in a hurry to get rid of me, aren't you?' He laughed. 'Okay, I'll let you go. One more thing. Ali's mother told me very sadly that she saw you on the street one day and you hurried away without speaking to her.'

'I don't want to see anyone connected to Ali,' I said.

'Till recently all she knew was that Ali had killed a policeman. She had no idea it was your baba,' he continued. 'In fact, that second bit of news shocked her more than anything else. She liked you so much.'

'I must go now,' I said.

'Day after tomorrow, I'll come to the cafe with Ali's mother. Please come and see us,' he said and before I could reply, he was off running again.

The Shore of Comfort

I decided to go. I knew that I wasn't strong enough to not go. But I also prayed that something would happen to prevent me from going. Maybe, I hoped, I would suddenly be called in for a live show or maybe I would get sick and not be able to get out of bed. Maybe the police would arrest me. Or perhaps, I would get hit by a car and die.

I didn't used to be like this. I have never hesitated to speak my mind or do what I wanted. It wasn't my style to consider if someone would be annoyed or hurt by my actions. But now, all I could do was think of how my actions affected other people.

Since none of those obstacles that I desired so much presented themselves, I did go to the cafe. I had nothing to say to Ali's mother. I would sit silently in front of her, I thought. I would express the anger I felt towards Ali. I would glower at her, pretending if need be that Sippy auntie was sitting in front of me.

The old man was waiting for me in the street. He came running to me as soon as I got out of the taxi. 'I knew you would come,' he said. 'Human goodness is stronger than any divine miracle.'

'I have to leave soon. I only came because you asked me to. You are as old as my grandfather and I didn't want to say no,' I said sternly. I found some confidence in that sternness and decided to keep it up till I left.

'Certainly, you may leave soon,' he replied. 'But I do have a surprise for you.'

I walked into the backyard with him expecting to meet Ali's mother. But instead, waiting for me were the String Walkers! Nazar, Farah, Roger, Sophia, Ifran and Salman. The moment I saw them, I felt my clouds of anger melt. I don't know why – but that is how I had felt when I saw them the other day in Taya Ghar as well. I did not share very deep friendships with any of them. The only thing that brought us all together was music. I was closer to Aisha auntie and Farhana, and even to my companions in Cattle Class. But when I saw the String Walkers, I felt a comfort that I did not feel in any of my other friendships.

But when they saw me, they seemed stunned, as if they had seen a ghost. For a moment I thought that my presence was not welcome.

Then Farah came up and took my hand in hers. 'What happened, Sameera? You look terrible. Were you sick? You were so beautiful. Even that day when we came to see you at home, you looked so much better,' she said sadly, hugging me. I touched my face, wonderingly. What was she talking about? Maybe this was her way of offering condolences, I thought. But one by one, everyone in the group, even Nazar who had no interest in such topics, confirmed that my appearance had changed drastically. It had been days since I had looked into a mirror or put on any make-up.

'Wasn't I right? See how tired she looks? Only you guys can bring her back to her old self. If not you guys, then your music,' the old man said. 'Play some nice songs for her. That will bring her some peace of mind.'

I have no idea where the next one hour went. As Nazar, Salman, Farah and Roger played, I bobbed on waves of music towards a shore of peace. A fragment of music is better than a thousand prayers. In music, we meet God.

'How do you feel now?' the old man asked.

'Comforted,' I said. No other word could have expressed what I felt.

'That day when I saw you here on your own I decided to bring everyone together. But I didn't know it would happen so fast.' The old man was full of glee at his success.

'When chacha said we must all bring Sameera back to life, there was no question about it. If we can't stand with our friends, what is the point of life?' Salman said.

'We knew that a String Walkers' gathering would bring you more happiness than some empty words of condolence. That's why we decided to set aside all quarrels and get back together.'

'I don't know how to thank you for your love.'

'The best way to express gratitude is to recognize the sorrows of other people,' Farah said.

I cried again. They left after asking me to worry less, eat well, get sleep, and practise a lot. They were eager to see the old Sameera, the lively radio jockey. Even though they offered to drop me off, the old man insisted that he would.

'Are you planning to walk all the way like you did that day?' I asked him.

'But of course! Why would I say no to an opportunity to walk with a pretty young woman?' He laughed.

'Oh, so now your true colours come out. You don't think you are a bit too old for this stuff?' I said sternly.

'You see, that's the difference between men and women. As far as you are concerned, what's the point of romance after fifty? Whereas we keep going, for about five minutes even after death.' He started getting up to leave.

'You think I don't know. Nowadays, I can't talk to a man without the conversation becoming about sex. We might start talking about religion, then maybe move on to football, and still end with a discussion on sex. Or begin with politics, continue on to cricket, and then move on to sex. You men have the same one-track mind,' I said as we walked.

'Some men seem to be under the impression that a lone woman is like a cow on the street, public property. The other day, someone at the office proposed to me. Did I want to be his second wife? For a few days I had been noticing his shenanigans around me, but then I thought maybe I had got too suspicious. So when he approached me and laid the matter out, I was shocked. An old man of forty-seven years, but he said he couldn't go to sleep unless I was beside him, warming the bed. I wanted to ask him, "Should I nurse you to sleep as well?" I would have given him a piece of my mind, but he was my supervisor. I came back to my table and sat there bursting with anger. As if I had any peace of mind otherwise, and then on top of it, this disgusting old man wants to romance me! I decided to teach him a lesson. So I went back to his office and said, "Sir, since you like me so much, why don't we be friends?" The bewakoof fell for that. He got emotional and said, "Yes, that's what I want, your friendship." So now he picks up my calls at any godforsaken time of the night. When I want to get back at him, I call him and say, "You monkey, where are you? I am eating ice-cream, come and join me," or I tease him, "If you come now, you can have some snacks with me." And he whines like a dog, "Darling, she's at home. I'll come another day."' I said with contempt in my voice.

'Women can make their besotted lovers do anything, from kissing their dirty dogs to dancing like monkeys.' He laughed.

'It's fun to string along these old men. There are younger ones too, but the poor kids are simply trying to figure out what romance is all about. So I am not too cruel with them. But if I get a chance to play some pranks on these gross old guys, I will take it. They don't deserve any sympathy from me.'

'Please leave this poor old man alone. I promise you that I am not up to any tricks.'

We both laughed. It had been days since I had talked openly with someone and laughed so much. I could feel the old Sameera returning.

That day too he took me all the way home.

'You now know the pain of losing someone beloved. So,

can you imagine the fate of a woman who lost three of the most loved men in her life?' he asked as we were parting.

At first I didn't understand who he was talking about. I screwed my face into a question mark.

'A woman like that would not be able to bear even a single angry glance from you. That's why I didn't bring her today. But now I have more faith in you. You both should meet sooner rather than later . . .'

He left then, after giving me something to think about and be distressed about.

A Woman's Life

That's how I started thinking about her life. Even that day when I saw her in person, I had not sensed the intensity of her life's experiences. The day I had gone to see Ali's uncle with Ali, I had seen a woman writing slogans on the wall. I had wondered what she wanted and why she wanted to incite the men in her life to protest. I didn't realize then that women like her walked on roads of embers. Their life was an endless wait for the husband kidnapped by the police, the missing brother, the son who had been imprisoned. Women who could not sleep because of the fire in their chest. Ali's mother was one of those women, battered by fate. Her oldest son had died on the street even as she was waiting for her missing husband. And just as that grief had probably begun to subside, her second son had been imprisoned for murder. What did she want from life any more? Perhaps an answer to the question, why me, why again and again?

That night I decided that I must indeed see her, as the old man had suggested. A couple of days later, after I got off from work, I went in search of him and asked him to take me to her. When he heard that, he stood up and praised me, 'That's wonderful, my child. I am so proud of you. I know this comes from deep inside your heart and not because I pressured you. That's why I said I have bottomless faith in human goodness. We'll go see her this week. She will be very happy to see you.'

We decided on a date for meeting Ali's mother. But that night taya called me to his room. We had not talked for a while and I had not asked him anything more about the reward from the government.

'The government is going to release your reward soon. All the paperwork is ready.' Taya didn't bother to make any small talk first.

I was surprised. Till then, he had spoken of it as 'our reward,' or the 'family reward'. Perhaps one of my other uncles had dissuaded him from that stance or maybe he had convinced Sippy auntie that they deserved no part in it.

'Good. That will be a comfort for us. Ma had mentioned several loans back home. At least we can repay those now,' I said.

'Along with that reward, the government has made another proposal,' taya added. I looked at him wondering what this new proposal was. After a long silence, he continued.

'The government will take care of all your ma's expenses till her death. The government will also take care of you kids, till you and Saima get married, and till Salman gets a job. Perhaps no one else in this country has been given such great benefits. You must understand how much the government and His Majesty valued your baba . . .'

What a miracle! Neither ma nor I could have even dreamed of it. Many nights ma had cried – how will I run the house without baba's income? I had returned to my own job after three months because I wanted her to stop fretting about money. This news would make ma very happy. A government allowance is a form of security. Ma would not have to depend on anyone. I felt grateful to the government and His Majesty for not forgetting poor ma. Strong emotions stirred in me.

'But the government has some conditions and you will have to agree to those,' taya said.

'What conditions? Whatever they are, I'll agree. Anything for ma,' I said.

'You have to quit the radio job and leave the country.'

I stared at him uncomprehendingly. 'Why?'

'I don't know. But that's what they want. I, too, was surprised when I first heard this condition. I have been thinking about it for the last two days. How could I ask you to leave a job that you love so much? I can understand your confusion. But then I thought, after all, it will help your mother. And perhaps you could find some other job in our own country. So, on the whole I think the smart thing is to agree to this condition.'

He did not look me in the face as he spoke. I had nothing to say for a minute. What was the connection between an allowance for ma and my job?

'Taya, you are so influential. Couldn't you ask them why they have this condition?'

'Certain decisions in this country cannot be questioned, my child. Whether we see the rationale behind them or not, we must obey them.'

'I have no regrets about leaving my job for ma's sake. But I have some concern about not even knowing why I have to. Till I get an explanation, I cannot quit my job,' I said in a firm voice.

'Sure, you can say that to me,' taya said. 'But between now and when I have to go back to them with your decision, give this some deep thought. Opportunities are like shooting stars. No use looking back and wishing you had caught them. You know that your radio job is here today, gone tomorrow. And our very existence in this country is a question in itself. So I don't understand why you are overthinking this proposal.'

'Well, if this proposal is in honour of baba's service to the country, I simply don't see why I have to leave my job and go back. And I suppose I have a small brain, but I do have some trouble saying yes to things I don't understand. You are welcome to consider it folly.'

'Beti, I have no interest in winning this argument. I am just the middleman here. The country has given you an offer. You can accept or refuse. The decision is yours.'

He stood up to indicate that the conversation was over.

'You have time until tomorrow evening. So let me know by then.' He opened the bedroom door for me and I saw Sippy auntie slinking away from behind the door like a cat.

I had a flash of understanding then. Something was rotten. Move carefully, I said to myself.

Street Lights

I went straight to bhupoma's room. That's where I always went to understand what was really going in Taya Ghar. 'Where have you been? I barely see you around,' bhupoma scolded me lovingly as I walked in.

'Did you hear, bhupoma? baba's reward from the government will be released soon. Taya just told me,' I said.

'Yes, I heard. A house without a man is a small hell. I hope the money saves you from that hell,' she said.

'But there were so many people with claims to that money until recently in Taya Ghar. What happened to all those claims?'

'Will you tell me the honest truth about something else?' bhupoma asked me.

'Honesty is my policy. That's in fact my problem,' I answered. 'Ask away.'

'Have you really decided to forgive Ali?'

'Ali?' I leaned forward like a question mark, surprised.

'Oh really. How many Alis do you know anyway? And how many whom you have to forgive?'

'Bhupoma, who's been filling your head with all this nonsense? I have not even thought of such a thing.'

'Well, the whole city is talking about this. We hear that his mother came to see you, that you are getting together

244

all the paperwork for the courts. If there's any truth to all this, beti, your father will never forgive you.' For the first time in her life, bhupoma seemed annoyed with me.

'I don't understand why the entire city is hounding me like this. What have I done to deserve this?' I was almost about to cry. 'I have done nothing, bhupoma.'

'That's what everyone in this family is hoping, beti. Already, we are under suspicion. Please don't get all the men fired. That's all I have to say.'

I sat with her for a while before returning to my room. Living in constant fear, Taya Ghar had concocted this conspiracy theory, I supposed. I didn't give it any more thought.

But the next day when I was sitting in the studio canteen, an RJ from Hit Arabia came up to me and took my hand. 'You have made a good decision. Allah will reward your generosity.'

I was taken aback. But she continued, 'All of us in this studio know that Ali is a good guy. Yes, he made a mistake at a time when the whole country was going mad. You have a big heart. Allah will certainly reward you.'

I stared at her helplessly.

That evening, on the way home, the car driver also asked me about it. In fact, he didn't just ask, he advised that I retract that decision immediately and avoid giving the government the impression that foreigners like us supported the protesters.

Later that evening I was walking in the souk when a few chachas I knew came out of their shops to talk to me. Some of them thought it was a good idea, others were against it.

I couldn't figure out how the gossip had started. Then I wondered if it was the old man. I called him that night to ask.

'You know that the government will issue a decision about Ali next week? They are almost certainly going to order capital punishment. One of the bloggers in the city wrote a post titled, "Should Sameera forgive Ali?" It went viral. Tens of thousands commented on it, both for and against. So that's where all the gossip is coming from. You know people, they will always find something or the other to talk about. Don't take it seriously. But remember that you are going through some of the most decisive moments of your life. You are bearing a burden that is much heavier than a woman as young as you should be bearing. But if you get through these days, you win. Do what feels infinitely right. There will be a thousand naysayers. Don't be tempted. Be steadfast . . .'

The old bookworm surprised me again. I felt inspired by his words. I thanked God for him. He was like a lamp lighting my way forward.

Without my knowledge, I seemed to have arrived at a decisive moment in my life. What was infinitely right? I asked myself. Ali getting punished or Ali escaping? Would baba be happy if Ali died? If Ali was forgiven, wouldn't it be tantamount to encouraging those who murder innocents? What made him do it – a lifetime of hatred or a moment's madness? Should I just leave him to his fate, whatever it was? Or should I actively try to change it? Why does this country want me to leave its shores? Should I accept the reward and the pension and leave or should I refuse it and stay here? What was the smart thing to do? What did I want to do? What would God want me to do? A thousand questions and a thousand answers.

Everything we have experienced in life goes into what we think of as right and wrong, isn't that so, Javed? Our family vocation is war, but we are Muslims and the lessons of Islam have shaped me. The Islam I learned is an Islam of goodness and patience. The Prophet I follow was a man who had forgiven his enemy Hind, who ate the liver of the Prophet's beloved uncle Hamza. I don't know how Islam became a religion of hatred and anger for Ali and his friends. Who taught him to interpret Islam like that? It was not any outsider's work. Insiders were responsible for it. A person's morality doesn't develop by itself, it is nourished by society. But if that is so, society was responsible for Ali's crime.

The society of Prophet Muhammad's time did not criticize him for forgiving Hind. But today if I decide to forgive Ali, a thousand of the Prophet's followers in this age would point their fingers at me. They would brand me as someone who betrayed her father, her family and her country. What should I do? Where would I find the strength to do the right thing?

CCTV

I went to see Ali's mother, just as I had decided, ignoring all the blaming and shaming this would earn me. Our meeting took place in a small Lebanese restaurant near the northern gate of the souk. The two of us sat across the table from each other, sipping our kahwas. She didn't ask me anything and I didn't say anything. Some silences are more meaningful than thousands of long sentences. I could sense her burning heart. She must have felt the ache inside me. When we left after that meeting, there was some comfort in our souls.

That night taya called me to his room for another talk. I thought he would ask me about my response to the government's offer and that I would tell him whatever happened, I would refuse. I may be bold but I had never disobeyed him before, but today, I thought, it would be necessary.

But he didn't bring up any of that. In fact, he did not even acknowledge me when I came in. Like a bureaucrat, he was busy on his computer. I waited for several minutes. I almost went back to my room. But I knew that would hurt him deeply. Even then, I held him in great affection and respect.

After some time, he turned the laptop around to face me. 'Take a look,' he said before leaving the room. I stared at the screen, surprised. It was a video taken from a CCTV camera. I sat down to watch.

A woman, not more than thirty years old, was sitting against a wall. From the way she was sitting, it's clear that she was exhausted. Someone not pictured was asking her to stand up and she tried a few times. But she couldn't. After each attempt, she looked up helplessly.

A few minutes later, a man in a black outfit entered the scene. There were three or four police officers accompanying him. From their uniforms, it was clear they were very high-ranking officers. But it was not clear who the man in black was. He circled the woman who was lying in a heap by now. When he turned the corner, I could see his face. When I recognized it, fear crawled up my spine like a snake. It was none other than His Majesty.

He walked around the woman a few times to take a good look at her, occasionally kicking her. She spat back at him, with all the energy she could muster for a final response. And though the spit only fell back on her own face, there was so much defiance and contempt in that gesture.

A chair was brought and His Majesty sat on it. The police officers stood around him in a semicircle as if they were watching a show. Another policeman brought a big framed photo to His Majesty. For some time he stared at the photo. Then he commanded that the woman be brought forward. Pointing at the photo, he asked her some questions. Then he threw the photo on the floor and shouted at her. The force of his shouting made him rise halfway from his chair. I saw the photo as it lay on the ground. It was a picture of His Majesty. The glass frame had shattered.

That's when I understood who the woman was. His Majesty asked her to stamp on the photo. But the woman merely fell down, her frail body slipping through the policemen's hands.

Then, two policemen tore her clothes off. Even though she resisted by holding on to her dress and rolling into a ball, within a few minutes she only had her underwear on. Another policeman brought a whip and started lashing her. When he whipped her back, she turned and lay on her back. Then he whipped her chest and she turned away from him. The beatings continued much longer than anyone could bear to watch. Currents of blood were running down her light skin. A policeman tore the hook off her bra. Another one kicked her bra off her body, as if it were a dead bat. She lay there helplessly without any strength left. Two young policemen came and lifted her up by her feet and threw her back on the floor. Her back hit the floor with a loud thud and she writhed in pain. Two other policemen lifted her by her feet again and then held her underwear by its sides. Her body fell on the floor naked.

For a few minutes the screen simply showed her bloody body lying on the floor. I thought the video had ended but the time stamp kept running. There was more to come.

Then His Majesty got off his chair and started jumping on her. He was not the ruler of a country any more; he was like a four-year-old jumping on a bed. Except for one thing – his face was full of the rage he felt towards the woman who had stamped on his picture in front of journalists. In the end, he poked the sharp heel of his shoe into her buttock. Her body jerked once in pain and then lay still. His Majesty spat on her face twice before leaving with his entourage. The video ended there. Taya's laptop screen filled with blackness. I stared at it and felt it entering my own body as a kind of numbness. I fainted deep into that numbness.

The Trial

I was travelling through a tunnel of light. The more I travelled, the lighter I felt. I was filled with a kind of ecstasy that I had never known before. I was moving closer and closer to the source of this beautiful light. All I wanted was to merge with that light. But suddenly I fell, like a flower falling off its stem, and returned to my body.

I opened my eyes. Aisha auntie was sitting next to me. Sippy auntie, taya, my chachas and mamus were standing around. They sprinkled some water on my face and brought me some lemon juice to drink. I felt a heavy sadness inside my chest. Wherever I had been just now, that's where I wanted to be. That was the sweetest experience of my life and they had pulled me out of it and brought me back here.

I sat up in the chair. Though my head started spinning, I found my balance. 'She is all right,' taya said, 'you can all return to your rooms.'

Farhana came rushing into the room just then. 'Why are you all punishing her like this? Let her get some rest,' she said.

Sippy auntie had been waiting for a provocation like that. Everything she wanted to yell at me, she started yelling at Farhana. And Farhana yelled back, with even more fervour than I had ever had. I watched her in awe. She had grown up in front of my eyes. She had learned to state her opinions without fear. It was as if a butterfly had emerged from a pupa. I hoped that she would fly high. Taya scolded her and told her to return to her room. That made her turn on him. She was young. She did not differentiate between taya and the others. She simply did not know how to measure the goodness in each person and give them their due.

I grabbed her hand and shook my head, don't. She left the room. When you see someone else making the same mistake you have made, then you realize exactly how bad it is. Taya was the head of this family. He had helped everyone in the family build their life here. Even now, as he stood in my way, it was not simply for his own survival, it was for the future of this family and each person in it. I could not pretend otherwise. Even as I fought for my own truth, I had to protect him.

Once again, it was just taya and me in the room.

'I know you are tired,' he said. 'But we don't have any time left. That is why I want you to stay back and finish this conversation. Now it is decision time. What do you have to say?'

'Taya, why did you show me this video?' I asked.

'He who knows Farsi is obviously educated,' he said. 'You are intelligent. You know why I showed you that video.'

'Did you think it would scare me?'

'No, I have not misunderstood you. But still, I felt that it was my responsibility to show you that video. Tomorrow, I don't want to feel guilty for not having done enough.'

'Well, this is my answer – I am refusing the government's offer.'

'What nonsense!' taya rose from his chair. 'Your selfishness and arrogance will destroy every bit of happiness this family has. You only think of yourself.'

'I do not understand why I have to leave this country,' I said, spelling out each syllable.

'Because they know you will bring harm to the country, that's why.'

'Harm to the country? What are they imagining, that I will bomb the City?'

'Don't think we don't know that you've been meeting those traitors and plotting.'

'Until this moment, I hadn't decided what to do in the matter of Ali. Well, now I have my decision. Whatever the price, I will save him from death.'

Taya slapped me. 'How dare you? Who do you think you are to spit on my brother's blood?' At that moment, he looked like the police officer he was.

'If killing someone would bring my baba back to life, yes, I would join you. But what is the point of all this, taya?'

'Yes, this argument has been put forward whenever it's been necessary to spare a murderer. It sounds logical, doesn't it? But all it does is manipulate us, exploit the humanity inside us. The point of punishment is not to bring anyone back to life. The point is to warn future criminals. When you decide to let one murderer go, you are encouraging a thousand murderers. It is a crime against society.'

'What do you want me to do, taya?'

'Stop taking decisions on your own and interfering with the course of law. Know that the rulers of this country have their own interests at heart and they will go to any extreme to protect those interests. Remember that we are immigrants and we don't have any rights and whatever we do have is a gift from these rulers. Do not anger them. Stop worrying about justice and injustice, let them do what they want in their own country. The pain we feel now is simply a price we pay for a better tomorrow.'

I sat there in silence with my head bowed. Slowly the room started filling with the different faces of my Taya Ghar family. Sippy auntie, Aisha auntie, bhupo, Khalid chacha, other uncles and aunts . . . they all crowded into the room. I knew that they were all begging for my mercy. Someone called my name, 'Sameera . . .' That voice was thick with all of Taya Ghar's aspirations and hopes. Dear God . . . the heaviness I felt in my chest then. Even if the skies and mountains had fallen down on my shoulders, the weight would have been far less. I prayed to Allah, please give me the strength I need to face this trial.

In the most trying moments of your life, do only that you know to be absolutely right. Thousands of people will approach you and offer thousands of opinions. Do not be influenced, do not give into temptations. Stand steadfast in truth. You will win.

The words of the old man from the cafe rang in my ears. I stood steadfast in my truth.

Afterword

Sameera Parvin

It's natural for a reader to wonder – what happened afterwards? And after that? And after that? You could keep asking this question. And I could keep answering. But a novel has to end somewhere. And this is where I have decided to end it. It was a decision Javed and I took together. A writer's choice and an editor's judgement. But here are a few things you would like to know.

The government released the reward money in honour of baba but it was divided between the members of Taya Ghar. We were told that a share was invested in ma's name, but I haven't seen any signs of that investment. Never mind. We are happy to let go of this blood money.

Taya was demoted at work. That drove Sippy auntie nearly mad. Taya had to take a long leave to help care for her. They went to Pakistan so she could get better.

Three days after taya left, I was placed under house arrest. I was not allowed to have any contact with the outside world. Two Syrian policemen stood guard outside my door, like a pair of hunting dogs, to make sure that I could not leave. But one day, bhupoma smuggled in a cellphone in her underwear when she brought me food. I did not use it for local calls because I did not want it to be traced. But I used it to access the Internet to get in touch with Javed and let

257

him know how I was trapped. He wanted to come to the City immediately but I stopped him. What does he know of this place? I believe that this house arrest will end soon and I will be deported. I want to leave this country before this country hears about the novel I wrote.

Perhaps the old man and my other friends think that I left the country secretly to avoid any involvement in Ali's case. I have no way of correcting their misapprehension. I hope they can forgive me.

As of this moment I am writing this, there is no verdict in Ali's case. But it has been already decided and I don't think anyone can change it. I pray that his mother will be able to bear the grief that lies in wait for her.

My gratitude to all those who loved me and tolerated me. To my friends in Orange Radio, the Mafia in Tunes Malayalam. To Taya Ghar which gave me its best and its worst. To bhupoma and Farhana for standing by me. To String Walkers. Ali, who threw his life into the sacrificial fires. And baba, where do I begin to thank you.

Javed, when I began this story I assured you that it would not end in tragedy. Even at this point, I would like to believe that. Even though I am standing on a cliff right now, somehow I am sure that I will not fall into the abyss. The pain will go away. The losses will no longer hurt. Joy will return. Life will go back to what it was. That is my hope.

Dear friend, for remembering me in my time of need, for listening to this story with an open heart, here is a doughnut from me! (I hope that this small joke will remind you of the old Sameera, the one I hope to recapture soon.)

Yes, today, I am opening the door to a new life.

Translator's Note
Benyamin

It was by accident that this book ended up in my hands. I was working in a foreign country then. One evening, I was invited to deliver the Che Guevara memorial lecture at an anti-war meeting organized by a cultural organization. After the lecture, my old friend Biju Menon introduced me to Mr Pratap, a Malayali journalist from Canada. He was also friendly with various other writer friends of mine such as Jayan K.C., John Ilamatha, Nirmala, Donna Mayura, Maya and Indira Banerjee. Pratap told me that he was in the City to conduct a market study for some multinational company and that he was interviewing people from different walks of life. He wanted a little time with me as well. So that day we got coffee together and talked about the City and the latest political developments. At some point, Pratap asked if I was interested in writing a novel about the City. I expressed my reluctance. To be honest, I was afraid of the consequences. That was more or less the end of our conversation.

Not long afterwards, I left the City for other reasons and moved back to Kerala. My goals were to travel widely, participate in literary events, read a lot and recover from the intense experience of writing and publishing five novels. I had no plans to write another one.

Around then, I got a call from Thiruvananthapuram, from my dear friend and well-known novelist V. J. James. He was calling to say that a visiting friend of his was eager to see me and if I had some time in the next week I should stop by Thiruvananthapuram. Luckily I was heading that way in three days for a book festival. I promised James that I would see them then. We met in a coffee shop in Vazhuthacaud. The friend was none other than Pratap. I hadn't expected a reunion like that. It seems they knew each other well because his sister and James had been classmates.

Pratap had proposed a project to James. He had been wanting to write a novel in Malayalam about his experiences in the City. But after all his days abroad, he was not confident about his use of the language. So he had approached James to ask if he could be a ghostwriter. But since James was busy writing his novel *Nireeshwaran*, he refused and instead suggested my name. Pratap must have been surprised by the coincidence of hearing my name after our chance meeting abroad.

Although Pratap argued that ghostwriting was not a new thing and that lots of writers made money that way, I dismissed that idea straight away. After all, I had not nurtured my writing so that I could write somebody else's novel. I owned the patent to my writing. I suppose I was a bit arrogant. We parted without reaching an agreement.

As I was leaving, he gave me a book. You couldn't call it a book actually. It was a photocopy. 'Remember how you were hesitant to write a novel about the City? Read this. Maybe your heart will murmur that this is the book you should have written,' he added sarcastically.

That's how I got hold of Sameera Parvin's *A Spring without Fragrance*. I think Pratap's parting shot found its aim. I read it in two days. Pratap was right. It was the novel I would have written if I had had the guts to write it. I pitied myself for not writing it. The novel drew me into its orbit.

We are hard-wired to share the good that happens to us. If we see a good movie, we want to tell a few people about it. If we hear a good song, we want our friends to listen to it. What's the point of making delicious food if we don't feed it to our loved ones? And when we are in love, we want to declare it to the entire world. A good book is like that. If we read a book that shakes us, we have to share that experience. Soon I was obsessed enough to ask Pratap to seek permission from the book's editors to translate it. That's when Pratap told me that he had already obtained the permission.

I begged Pratap to release the right to translate. I was infatuated with the novel. Pratap twisted my arm a bit. 'If you can bring my novel to life, then you can have this permission.'

We had many long discussions. We fought and we made up. Pratap came to India a couple of times. Finally Pratap came around to seeing the issue from my perspective. Whoever the story belongs to, the language is the writer's. You cannot sell language. We decided in the end that I would write Pratap's story as a novel. He had three conditions.

1. He would choose the title of the novel
2. He would dedicate the novel as he chose
3. The characters' names could not be changed.

I had no trouble agreeing to those three conditions. That's how I became Sameera Parvin's translator. And that's also how I came to write a novel that I hadn't expected to write – *Al Arabian Novel Factory*. Thank you, Pratap.

Benyamin

A Preview Chapter from
Al Arabian Novel Factory

Coming out in 2019

Jasmine Days *and* Al Arabian Novel Factory *are twin novels, set against the backdrop of the Arab Spring. In* Al Arabian, *Pratap, a Canadian writer of Indian origin, sets out to assist a well-known novelist in researching a book set in the Middle East. He arrives with a team of researchers in the City, just as the protest movement is dying out. He also has a personal agenda – to find his old flame, Jasmine. Pratap slowly gets drawn into the City's politics and comes across Sameera's letters, which are eventually translated into English and published as* Jasmine Days.

In this preview chapter, Pratap has just landed in the City.

The first thing I did that day was rent a car. In any new place, mobility is the most important freedom to achieve.

At the car rental agency, I was surprised to see many Malayalis. At my apartment building too, the receptionist, the cleaning staff, the watchman, the pool operator – they were all Malayalis. The department stores I visited yesterday with my friend Bijumon had also been full of Malayalis. And now, at the car rental agency, a Malayali called Reji stood behind the desk.

Reji pushed me towards the big cars. The rental fees were half what they used to be, he said. He also pointed out that the big cars came equipped with a GPS, making the City much more navigable. But I didn't want to sit behind the wheel and follow a machine's orders. I wanted the streets of the City to myself. I wanted to get lost. I wanted to go down a wrong street, return and wonder where to go next. I don't like streets that have all the right answers.

I finally rented a cheap car of Japanese make. Then I turned to the task of getting to know the City and its people.

'How is business?' I asked Reji.

'Very bad. No one comes here any more. You should have seen how it was here in the olden days. Tourists everywhere! In a single weekend I used to rent out two to three hundred cars.' Reji sounded distressed. 'I don't know how much longer I can go on like this. It's been seven months since I got my salary. I forget the last time I sent any money home. The landlord keeps asking for the rent and I have nothing to give him. I am just holding on, hoping things will get better.'

'But why? Why not look for another job?' I asked.

'What can I say. I have been here for fifteen years. I was here during the golden age of the City, and I enjoyed every bit of it. Now the City has fallen on bad times, but I just have to stick it out. Of course, I came here to make money. But this is my home now. All my friends are here. What's the point of thinking only about money? What kind of a life is that?'

I headed out with that question ringing in my head. I drove around aimlessly. I wanted to meet the City, to introduce myself to it. I went through long avenues and narrow galis. I passed shops and malls. I mapped the City's landmarks: Tripoli Hotel, Sana Fabrics, Baghdad Avenue, Tehran Carpets, Cairo Perfumes, Muscat Mall, Amman Tower. None of them seemed unfamiliar. I had roamed the city in my mind, holding Jasmine's hand. In reality, all I knew was that she lived in some corner of the City and worked for an insurance company. But still, I kept an eye out, expecting a miracle – that she would appear in front of me. From her Facebook photo, I knew the balcony of her flat, the peach-coloured paint on its walls, the flowerpot on one side. From an email, I knew that her flat faced a mosque with tall minarets. There was an almond tree near the spot where she waited for her bus. Whenever I saw an apartment building with balconies, or an almond tree, or the minarets of a mosque, I studied it eagerly.

Edwin arrived three days later and I went to meet him at the airport. He was coming from London, where he worked for the research team of the anonymous writer who had hired our firm. Barely twenty-five years old, he seemed a high-octane character. We had only exchanged a few emails, but he greeted me as if I were an old friend.

He told me that he was relatively new to the job. Prior to

this, he had helped research the life of horsemen in a village called Semeru Loang near the volcanic Mount Bramo in Indonesia. 'I was about to head to Italy to conduct research for a novel set in Renaissance churches, when this came up. I have always wanted to see the Arabian peninsula. So I was happy to jump ship.'

As we walked to the parking lot, Edwin introduced me to the woman with him. 'This is Asmo Andros from Budapest. Can we drop her off at her villa on the way?'

Asmo's villa was on an island called Palm Gardens, near the airport. It was clearly a wealthy community and as we drove past sea-facing villas, Asmo pointed towards another island. 'That's His Majesty's holiday palace. He visits once a year or so.'

'Oh no . . . poor little Majesty! That little hovel over there is what Arabs call a palace?' Edwin sniggered. 'Even an ordinary billionaire in my country would live in a much better house. And we don't even have any oil, we merely steal theirs.' I thought of some of the splendid Indian palaces. Even a zamindar in India lives in more glory than some of these Middle Eastern royals.

As she got out of the car, Asmo shook hands with me. Edwin got a long kiss. 'We just met on the flight,' he said on the way to our apartment. I was astonished. I had thought she was his long-time girlfriend.

'Asmo was sitting next to me on the flight. She was reading her book seriously, as if she was a professor. When I said hello, she gave me a grim "Hi" and went back to her book. I was miffed. What was this book she was reading when she could have been flirting with a blue-eyed stud like me? It was *In Praise of the Stepmother* by Mario Vargas Llosa. I have read some of his other stuff but not that one, so I had no idea what it was about. I should have known something was up because after reading each sentence, the grim professor lady smiled to herself.

'At some point, she fell asleep and I picked up the book from her lap and took a look at what she had been reading. I couldn't believe my eyes. It was a detailed description of a woman going wild with pleasure. Now I understood those smiles of hers. When she woke up, I was reading the book. She started laughing, and that's how we introduced ourselves to each other.

'Her family is from Lebanon, but when she was thirteen, and the Lebanese civil war was at its height, they moved to Budapest. Now she works for a bank in the City. When I told her that I was part of the research team of an internationally renowned writer, she got very excited. After that, we could not stop talking about writers and books. Why did Gabriel García Márquez punch Mario Vargas Llosa? Please could someone recover Sylvia Plath's lost novel? What was her theory about Edgar Allan Poe's mysterious death? Whom did I prefer, Roberto Bolano or María Amparo Escandón? Was Virginia Woolf a lesbian? Is it true that J.K. Rowling was writing the new Harry Potter? Where was Salman Rushdie hiding? Some day we must visit Orhan Pamuk's Museum of Innocence . . . This is what passes for small talk between book lovers. At some point, we were holding hands. It was a meeting of souls. So, you see, I feel doubly fortunate to be stepping into this city.'

For Edwin, the Middle East was a place of bloody legends and tales of terror. He thirsted to know what this region was really like, how it moved forward despite its storied past.

'People on our team were scared of this project,' he said, 'whereas I jumped at the opportunity to come here. With Saudi Arabia on one side and Iran on the other, I am not surprised they were scared. But I have always been curious about the City, about how it rose out of the dust like an enchanted land in a fairy tale.

'But mine is not just a journalist's interest or a European's curiosity,' he continued. 'I, too, have an old connection to the City. My great-grandfather George Martin Lease spent most of his youth here. Have you heard of Major Frank Holmes, who found the first oil reserves in this region? My great-grandfather was his best friend and a member of his prospecting team. They were both geologists. They met and bonded during the First World War, while working in the British Army's supply section. Both of them dreamed of oil. When they came to Iraq they were both convinced that there were oil deposits in the Middle East. As they stood on this soil, Frank Holmes turned to my great-grandfather and said, "I smell oil." After the war, they both left the army and switched to oil prospecting. Holmes had some experience looking for gold in South Africa and my great-grandfather had spent some time in the coal mines of India, but that was it. They wandered all over the Mesopotamian desert and the Persian peninsula sniffing for oil.

'Everyone discouraged them. Mocked them, in fact.

Imagine, oil in this savage land. But they were not quitters. They were both hardcore geologists and instinct told them there was a deep reservoir of oil somewhere underneath all that desert soil. Finally, they got some support from Eastern and General Syndicate Limited. Soon after that, they were able to find oil and prove that they were not just two crazy old men. They had started sometime in 1925 and it was in 1931 that they finally found oil. In the summer of 1932, the first oil well in the Middle East started production, changing the course of this region's history. My great-grandfather returned to London, happy with his discovery. He died soon after of cholera and disappeared from the history of oil, but Holmes lived till 1947. He was honoured for his discovery. They call him the "father of oil".

'Even four generations later, my family still talks proudly of George Martin Lease and his oil days. In our living room, we have displayed a photocopy of the original agreement between his company and the rulers of this land. As children, the moment we could piece words together, we tried to read that agreement. We read it like a fairy tale. We recited that agreement the way other kids sang "Twinkle Twinkle Little Star". Look, even now, it comes to me so easily . . .'

Sitting on the balcony of my room enjoying a beer, he recited: 'Agreement between Sheikh Al Khalifah of the one part, hereafter called "the Sheikh" and Eastern and General Syndicate Limited of the other part, hereafter called "the Company". The Sheikh grants to the company by these presents an exclusive exploration licence for a period not exceeding two years. From the date of this agreement hereby the company shall be entitled throughout the whole of the territory under his control to explore and search the surface of such territories to a depth not exceeding twenty feet for natural gas, petroleum asphalt and ozokerite, and enjoy the privileges set out in the first schedule to this agreement; he also undertakes on behalf of himself and his successors to grant to the company further exclusive licence and privileges, if the company shows to the satisfaction of the Sheikh, actions on the advice of the Political Resident in the Persian Gulf. Dated the Second of December 1925.'

There were two more members in our team but their arrival had been delayed again and again and their tickets had to be rebooked several times. 'You Canadians and Europeans don't know what visa problems are,' our project coordinator, Abdullah Janahi, told us. 'The two people we are waiting for are from Asian countries. They have to jump through hoops to get their visas.' I recalled how I had walked out of the airport after five minutes of visa processing while labourers from the Asian countries had been sent to stand in long lines as if they were cattle.

We could not wait for them indefinitely. It was time to start work. Edwin and I picked one of the four office spaces that Abdullah Janahi showed us. Of course, I had no idea where to begin. It's not as if we could simply waylay people on the street. And besides, who would want to bare their soul to strangers? Could the stories we gathered from newspapers and official documents be anything other than superficial? How far could a writer go with such research? Though Edwin was supposedly there to give us guidance, I couldn't bring myself to ask a much younger man for advice. Still, we often went out together. Edwin was enthralled at the idea of being in an Arab city. Everything he saw fuelled his enchantment. The man on the cycle with birdcages strapped behind him, the Bangladeshi migrant roasting peanuts by the side of the road, little Arab urchins who tailed us offering to sell us the latest cellphones at rock-bottom prices, donkey carts with oil tanks in them, women dressed from head to toe in black posing for selfies, the middle-aged man who spread out his prayer rug on the sidewalk and started praying – everything moved Edwin to wonder.

Whenever he saw an Arab in traditional robes, he stared as though he were in a dream. He thought of them as characters in some folk tale. 'I see bygone eras in their faces, Pratap.' That was his half-stupid, half-innocent explanation.

On some days, I wandered around the City on my own. I was not so much searching for authentic experiences to record as I was hoping to run into Jasmine. I longed to see her in the streets. During those wanderings, I met two acquaintances from my home town in India. I hadn't even known they lived here. But the person I desired did not appear.

I was seeing the City, of course. But I was not experiencing it. Like any other city, it seemed to wake up, go through the motions of the day, and go to sleep. The usual crowds, the usual rush hour. There were no signs of the protests that had recently taken place here. To think about the fear this city had inspired when I mentioned my travel plans! Sure, there was a curfew and that made life inconvenient. But that was it. Barely enough to fill a three-column newspaper article.

That weekend I went to the Malayali Samajam in the City with Bijumon. It was an elegant building with huge grounds. I could hear the sounds of a tennis match from its courts. The library was filled with readers. There was a seminar on 'Globalization and a Changing World'. It began with a speech thanking His Majesty for the opportunity to organize the seminar. This was followed by fierce speeches about how globalization was taking the form of neo-colonialism and the importance of defending democracy. I, too, was invited to speak but I declined. Someone muttered, 'What can a Canadian say about colonialism. He is probably all for globalization.' I did not respond to that. I had only pity for those who made speeches of political resistance after first thanking His Majesty.

By the time we left, it was almost midnight. Bijumon, his friend Raju Narayan and I got into my car and set out to find something to eat. Raju had once been an active member of the Communist Party of Kerala. Five years ago, when he was working at the district level of the party, he had taken a leave of absence to come to the City. 'I had some debts to repay. Afterwards, I just stayed on. That's how it goes in this city,' he said. 'It doesn't let go of you. The way I look at it, once life achieves a certain standard, that's socialism in action right there. At least I can say that socialism has been achieved in my own life. I've paid my debts and now I have some savings in the bank. So why should I return to my old life?'

On the way to the restaurant, we got caught in traffic. Several police vehicles stood ahead, their lights flashing. Fire engines with blaring alarms were driving down the sidewalk to cut through the traffic. I thought there must have been an accident. Though Bijumon and Raju told me not to, I got out of the car, unable to tamp down my newshound curiosity. Further up, after a few vehicles, I saw fire on the street. Maybe a car had caught fire? But when I got closer, I saw that a pile of tyres was blocking the road and had been set on fire. The police were trying to put out the fire. At the same time, lit torches were being hurled at the police from behind a nearby wall. The police were fighting back with tear gas bombs. I felt my own eyes suddenly tear up and ran back to the car.

Bijumon and Raju laughed at me. 'Told you so,' they mocked. 'We thought, why not let the Canadian learn the hard way?' Within fifteen minutes, the fires were put out and the traffic started moving again.

'Consider this a local Arab custom,' the communist leaned in from the back seat to inform me. 'This is how they celebrate their weekends. Some fire on the streets, some tear gas bombs. Maybe a few bullets to go around. On most weekends, a couple of them will get slaughtered. The next day, the corpses will get a grand burial. That's how they live. Don't dwell on it.'

I swallowed my anger and asked Raju, 'Have you ever tried to understand what the real issues are?'

'What's there to understand?' Raju asked, genuinely surprised. 'They are just a bunch of rowdies and religious fanatics. You have no idea, Mr Pratap, how peacefully and happily we foreigners lived here under His Majesty's rule. No country was more beautiful. And His Majesty looked on us as his own subjects. We had all the freedoms we could possibly want. We had churches and temples and gurdwaras and schools and bars and our own Malayali Samajam where we elected our own administration. In fact, Mr Pratap, the Communist Party of Kerala has a branch committee here. Every year we donate lakhs of rupees to the party fund in Kerala. I don't think we would have this much freedom even in a communist country. Still, these locals won't stop moaning about how they have no freedom. They keep crying for democracy.'

'Do you know why we are telling you all this?' Bijumon took up the conversation. 'Short-term visitors like you see all this noise in the streets and get scared and report that terrible things are happening here. And that's exactly what they want. Ruin the country's reputation. Destroy the economy. There is an international agenda behind all this. If this were happening back in India, they would all be dead. His Majesty is too good for this world, that's why they are still alive.'

That night we ate chicken tikka and lamb chops and beef kebab and hummus in a Lebanese restaurant. But I could not stomach it. When I returned to the apartment, I threw up. Along with all that roasted meat, there were some undigested words in my puddle of vomit.

juggernaut

THE APP FOR INDIAN READERS

Fresh, original books tailored for mobile and for India. Starting at ₹10.

juggernaut.in

CRAFTED
FOR MOBILE
READING

*Thought you would never read a book
on mobile? Let us prove you wrong.*

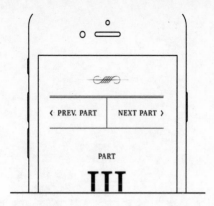

Beautiful Typography

The quality of print transferred to your mobile. Forget ugly PDFs.

Customizable Reading

Read in the font size, spacing and background of your liking.

AN EXTENSIVE LIBRARY

Including fresh, new, original Juggernaut books from the likes of Sunny Leone, Praveen Swami, Husain Haqqani, Umera Ahmed, Rujuta Diwekar and lots more. Plus, books from partner publishers and loads of free classics. Whichever genre you like, there's a book waiting for you.

DON'T
JUST READ;
INTERACT

We're changing the reading experience from passive to active.

Ask authors questions

Get all your answers from the horse's mouth.
Juggernaut authors actually reply to every
question they can.

Rate and review

Let everyone know of your favourite reads or
critique the finer points of a book – you will be
heard in a community of like-minded readers.

Gift books to friends

For a book-lover, there's no nicer gift than
a book personally picked. You can even
do it anonymously if you like.

Enjoy new book formats

Discover serials released in parts over
time, picture books including comics,
and story-bundles at discounted rates.
And coming soon, audiobooks.

4

LOWEST PRICES & ONE-TAP BUYING

Books start at ₹10 with regular discounts and free previews.

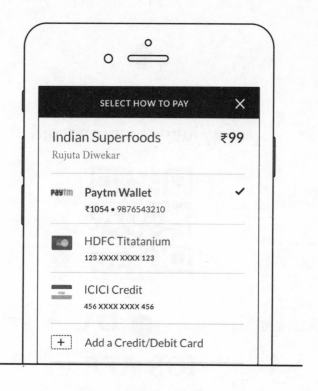

Paytm Wallet, Cards & Apple Payments

On Android, just add a Paytm Wallet once and buy any book with one tap. On iOS, pay with one tap with your iTunes-linked debit/credit card.

Click the QR Code with a QR scanner app
or type the link into the Internet browser
on your phone to download the app.

ANDROID APP

bit.ly/juggernautandroid

iOS APP

bit.ly/juggernautios

For our complete catalogue, visit www.juggernaut.in
To submit your book, send a synopsis and two
sample chapters to books@juggernaut.in
For all other queries, write to contact@juggernaut.in